The Bookshop

PENELOPE FITZGERALD has three grown-up
children, an economist, a Spanish teacher, and
a physiologist. The family used to live on a
Thames barge, which sank, but are now settled
in London and Somerset. *The Bookshop*, was
shortlisted for the Booker Prize in 1978. She
won the Prize the following year for *Offshore*,
and has since been shortlisted again in 1988 for
The Beginning of Spring, and in 1990 for *The Gate
of Angels*.

Penelope Fitzgerald

The Bookshop

Flamingo
An Imprint of HarperCollins*Publishers*

Flamingo
An Imprint of HarperCollins*Publishers*
77–85 Fulham Palace Road,
Hammersmith, London W6 8JB

First published by Flamingo 1989
9 8 7 6 5 4 3

First published by
Gerald Duckworth and Co. Ltd 1978

Set in Baskerville

Printed in Great Britain by
HarperCollins Manufacturing Glasgow

To an old friend

1

In 1959 Florence Green occasionally passed a night when she was not absolutely sure whether she had slept or not. This was because of her worries as to whether to purchase a small property, the Old House, with its own warehouse on the foreshore, and to open the only bookshop in Hardborough. The uncertainty probably kept her awake. She had once seen a heron flying across the estuary and trying, while it was on the wing, to swallow an eel which it had caught. The eel, in turn, was struggling to escape from the gullet of the heron and appeared a quarter, a half, or occasionally three-quarters of the way out. The indecision expressed by both creatures was pitiable. They had taken on too much. Florence felt that if she hadn't slept at all – and people often say this when they mean nothing of the kind – she must have been kept awake by thinking of the heron.

She had a kind heart, though that is not of much use when it comes to the matter of self-preservation. For more than eight years of half a lifetime she had lived at Hardborough on the very small amount of money her late husband had left her and had recently come to wonder whether she hadn't a duty to make it clear to herself, and possibly to others, that she existed in her own right. Survival was often considered all that could be asked in the cold and clear East Anglian air. Kill or cure, the inhabitants thought – either a long old age, or immediate consignment to the salty turf of the churchyard.

She was in appearance small, wispy and wiry, somewhat insignificant from the front view, and totally so from the back. She was not much talked about, not even in Hardborough, where everyone could be seen coming over the wide distances and everything seen was discussed. She made small seasonal changes in what she wore. Everybody knew her winter coat, which was the kind that might just be made to last another year.

In 1959, when there was no fish and chips in Hardborough, no launderette, no cinema except on alternate Saturday nights, the need of all these things was felt, but no one had considered, certainly had not thought of Mrs Green as considering, the opening of a bookshop.

'Of course I can't make any definite commitment on behalf of the bank at the moment – the decision is not in my hands – but I think I may say that there will be no objection in principle to a loan. The Government's word up to now has been restraint in credit to the private borrower, but there are distinct signs of relaxation – I'm not giving away any state secrets there. Of course, you'll have little or no competition – a few novels, I'm told, lent out at the Busy Bee wool shop, nothing significant. You assure me that you've had considerable experience of the trade.'

Florence, preparing to explain for the third time what she meant by this, saw herself and her friend, their hair in Eugene waves, chained pencils round their necks, young assistants of twenty-five years ago at Müller's in Wigmore Street. It was the stocktaking she remembered best, when Mr Müller, after calling for silence, read out with calculated delay the list of young ladies and their partners, drawn by lot, for the day's checking over. There were by no means enough fellows to go round, and she had been lucky to be paired, in 1934, with Charlie Green, the poetry buyer.

'I learned the business very thoroughly when I was a girl,' she said. 'I don't think it's changed in essentials since then.'

'But you've never been in a managerial position. Well,

8

–

there are one or two things that might be worth saying. Call them words of advice, if you will.'

There were very few new enterprises in Hardborough, and the notion of one, like a breath of sea air far inland, faintly stirred the sluggish atmosphere of the bank.

'I mustn't take up your time, Mr Keble.'

'Oh, you must allow me to be judge of that. I think I might put it in this way. You must ask yourself, when you envisage yourself opening a bookshop, what your objective really is. That is the first question needful to a business of any kind. Do you hope to give our little town a service that it needs? Do you hope for sizeable profits? Or are you, perhaps, Mrs Green, a jogger along, with little understanding of the vastly different world which the 1960s may have in store for us? I've often thought that it's a pity that there isn't some accepted course of study for the small business man or woman . . .'

Evidently there was an accepted course for bank managers. Launched on the familiar current, Mr Keble's voice gathered pace, with the burden of many waters. He spoke of the necessity of professional book-keeping, systems of loan repayment, and opportunity costs.

'. . . I would like to put a point, Mrs Green, which in all probability has not occurred to you, and yet which is so plain to those of us who are in a position to take the broader view. My point is this. *If over any given period of time the cash inflow cannot meet the cash outflow, it is safe to predict that money difficulties are not far away.*'

Florence had known this ever since her first payday, when, at the age of sixteen, she had become self-supporting. She prevented herself from making a sharp reply. What had become of her resolve, as she crossed the market place to the bank building, whose solid red brick defied the prevailing wind, to be sensible and tactful?

'As to the stock, Mr Keble, you know that I've been given

the opportunity of buying most of what I need from Müller's, now that they're closing down.' She managed to say this resolutely, although she had felt the closure as a personal attack on her memories. 'I've had no estimate for that as yet. And as to the premises, you agreed that £3,500 was a fair price for the freehold of the Old House and the oyster shed.'

To her surprise, the manager hestitated.

'The property has been standing empty for a long time now. That is, of course, a matter for your house agent and your solicitor – Thornton, isn't it?' This was an artistic flourish, a kind of weakness, since there were only two solicitors in Hardborough. 'But I should have thought the price might have come down further . . . The house won't walk away if you decide to wait a little . . . deterioration . . . damp . . .'

'The bank is the only building in Hardborough which isn't damp,' Florence replied. 'Working here all day may perhaps have made you too demanding.'

'. . . and then I've heard it suggested – I'm in a position where I can say that I understand it may have been suggested – that there are other uses to which the house might be put – though of course there is always the possibility of a re-sale.'

'Naturally I want to reduce expenses to a minimum.' The manager prepared to smile understandingly, but spared himself the trouble when Florence added sharply 'But I've no intention of re-selling. It's a peculiar thing to take a step forward in middle age, but having done it I don't intend to retreat. What else do people think the Old House could be used for? Why haven't they done anything about it in the past seven years? There were jackdaws nesting in it, half the tiles were off, it stank of rats. Wouldn't it be better as a place where people could stand and look at books?'

'Are you talking about culture?' the manager said, in a voice half way between pity and respect.

'Culture is for amateurs. I can't run my shop at a loss. Shakespeare was a professional!'

It took less than it should have done to fluster Florence, but at least she had the good fortune to care deeply about something. The manager replied soothingly that reading took up a great deal of time. 'I only wish I had more time at my disposal. People have quite wrong ideas, you know, about the bank's closing hours. Speaking personally, I enjoy very little leisure in the evenings. But don't misunderstand me, I find a good book at my bedside of incalculable value. When I eventually retire I've no sooner read a few pages than I'm overwhelmed with sleep.'

She reflected that at this rate one good book would last the manager for more than a year. The average price of a book was twelve shillings and sixpence. She sighed.

She did not know Mr Keble at all well. Few people in Hardborough did. Although they were constantly told, by press and radio, that these were prosperous years for Britain, most of Hardborough still felt the pinch, and avoided the bank manager on principle. The herring catch had dwindled, naval recruitment was down, and there were many retired persons living on a fixed income. These did not return Mr Keble's smile or his wave out of the hastily wound-down window of his Austin Cambridge. Perhaps this was why he went on talking for so long to Florence, although the discussion was scarcely businesslike. Indeed it had reached, in his view, an unacceptably personal level.

Florence Green, like Mr Keble, might be accounted a lonely figure, but this did not make them exceptional in Hardborough, where many were lonely. The local naturalists, the reedcutter, the postman, Mr Raven the marshman, bicycled off one by one, leaning against the wind, the observed of all observers, who could reckon the time by their reappearance over the horizon. Not all of these solitaries even went out.

Mr Brundish, a descendant of one of the most ancient Suffolk families, lived as closely in his house as a badger in its sett. If he emerged in summer, wearing tweeds between dark green and grey, he appeared a moving gorse-bush against the gorse, or earth against the silt. In autumn he went to ground. His rudeness was resented only in the same way as the weather, brilliant in the morning, clouding over later, however much it had promised.

The town itself was an island between sea and river, muttering and drawing into itself as soon as if felt the cold. Every fifty years or so it had lost, as though careless or indifferent to such things, another means of communication. By 1850 the Laze had ceased to be navigable and the wharfs and ferries rotted away. In 1910 the swing bridge fell in, and since then all traffic had to go ten miles round by Saxford in order to cross the river. In 1920 the old railway was closed. The children of Hardborough, waders and divers all, had most of them never been in a train. They looked at the deserted LNER station with superstitious reverence. Rusty tin strips, advertising Fry's Cocoa and Iron Jelloids, hung there in the wind.

The great floods of 1953 caught the sea wall and caved it in, so that the harbour mouth was dangerous to cross, except at very low tide. A rowing-boat was now the only way to get across the Laze. The ferryman chalked up his times for the day on the door of his shed, but this was on the far shore, so that no one in Hardborough could ever be quite certain when they were.

After her interview with the bank, and resigned to the fact that everyone in the town knew that she had been there, Florence went for a walk. She crossed the wooden planks across the dykes, preceded as she tramped by a rustling and splashing as small creatures, she didn't know of what kind, took to the water. Overhead the gulls and rooks sailed confidently on the tides of the air. The wind had shifted and was blowing inshore.

Above the marshes came the rubbish tip, and then the rough fields began, just good enough for the farmers to fence. She heard her name called, or rather she saw it, since the words were blown away instantly. The marshman was summoning her.

'Good morning, Mr Raven.' That couldn't be heard either.

Raven acted, when no other help was at hand, as a kind of supernumerary vet. He was in the Council field, where the grazing was let out at five shillings a week to whoever would take it, and at the extreme opposite end stood an old chestnut gelding, a Suffolk Punch, its ears turning delicately like pegs on its round poll in the direction of the human beings in its territory. It held its ground suspiciously, with stiffened legs, against the fence.

When she got within five yards of Raven, she understood that he was asking for the loan of her raincoat. His own clothes were rigid, layer upon layer, and not removable on demand.

Raven never asked for anything unless it was absolutely necessary. He accepted that coat with a nod, and while she stood keeping as warm as she could in the lee of the thorn hedge, he walked quietly across the field to the intensely watching old beast. It followed every movement with flaring nostrils, satisfied that Raven was not carrying a halter, and refusing to stretch its comprehension any further. At last it had to decide whether to understand or not, and a deep shiver, accompanied by a sigh, ran through it from nose to tail. Then its head drooped, and Raven put one of the sleeves of the raincoat round its neck. With a last gesture of independence, it turned its head aside and pretended to look for new grass in the damp patch under the fence. There was none, and it followed the marshman awkwardly down the field, away from the indifferent cattle, towards Florence.

'What's wrong with him, Mr Raven?'

'He eats, but he's not getting any good out of the grass. His teeth are blunted, that's the reason. He tears up the grass, but that doesn't get masticated.'

'What can we do, then?' she asked with ready sympathy.

'I can fare to file them,' the marshman replied. He took a halter out of his pocket and handed back the raincoat. She turned into the wind to button herself into her property. Raven led the old horse forward.

'Now, Mrs Green, if you'd catch hold of the tongue. I wouldn't ask everybody, but I know you don't frighten.'

'*How* do you know?' she asked.

'They're saying that you're about to open a bookshop. That shows you're ready to chance some unlikely things.'

He slipped his finger under the loose skin, hideously wrinkled, above the horse's jawbone and the mouth gradually opened in an extravagant yawn. Towering yellow teeth stood exposed. Florence seized with both hands the large slippery dark tongue, smooth above, rough beneath, and, like an old-time whaler, hung gamely on to it to lift it clear of the teeth. The horse now stood sweating quietly, waiting for the end. Only its ears twitched to signal a protest at what life had allowed to happen to it. Raven began to rasp away with a large file at the crowns of the side teeth.

'Hang on, Mrs Green. Don't you relax your efforts. That's slippery as sin I know.'

The tongue writhed like a separate being. The horse stamped with one foot after another, as though doubting whether they all still touched the ground.

'He can't kick forwards, can he, Mr Raven?'

'He can if he likes.' She remembered that a Suffolk Punch can do anything, except gallop.

'Why do you think a bookshop is unlikely?' she shouted into the wind. 'Don't people want to buy books in Hardborough?'

'They've lost the wish for anything of a rarity,' said Raven, rasping away. 'There's many more kippers sold, for example, than bloaters that are half-smoked and have a more delicate flavour. Now you'll tell me, I dare say, that books oughtn't to be a rarity.'

Once released, the horse sighed cavernously and stared at them as though utterly disillusioned. From the depths of its noble belly came a brazen note, more like a trumpet than a horn, dying away to a snicker. Clouds of dust rose from its body, as though from a beaten mat. Then, dismissing the whole matter, it trotted to a safe distance and put down its head to graze. A moment later it caught sight of a patch of bright green angelica and began to eat like a maniac.

Raven declared that the old animal would not know itself, and would feel better. Florence could not honestly say the same of herself, but she had been trusted, and that was not an everyday experience in Hardborough.

2

The property which Florence had determined to buy had not been given its name for nothing. Although scarcely any of the houses, until you got out to the half-built council estate to the north-west, were new, and many dated from the eighteenth and nineteenth centuries, none of them compared with the Old House, and only Holt House, Mr Brundish's place, was older. Built five hundred years ago out of earth, straw, sticks and oak beams, the Old House owed its survival to a flood cellar down a flight of stone steps. In 1953 the cellar had carried seven foot of seawater until the last of the floods had subsided. On the other hand, some of the seawater was still there.

Inside was the large front room, the backhouse kitchen, and upstairs a bedroom under a sloping ceiling. Not adjoining, but two streets away on the foreshore, stood the oyster shed which went with the property and which she had hoped to use as a warehouse for the reserve stock. But it turned out that the plaster had been mixed, for convenience sake, with sand from the beach, and sea sand never dries out. Any books left there would be wrinkled with damp in a few days. Her disappointment, however, endeared her to the shopkeepers of Hardborough. They had all known better, and could have told her so. They felt a shift in the balance of intellectual power, and began to wish her well.

Those who had lived in Hardborough for some time also knew that her freehold was haunted. The subject was not avoided, it was a familiar one. The figure of a woman, for example, could sometimes be seen down at the landing-stage of the ferry, about twilight, waiting for her son to come back, although he had been drowned over a hundred years ago. But the Old House was not haunted in a touching manner. It was infested by a poltergeist which, together with the damp and an unsolved question about the drains, partly accounted for the difficulty in selling the property. The house agent was in no way legally bound to mention the poltergeist, though he perhaps alluded to it in the phrase *unusual period atmosphere*.

Poltergeists, in Hardborough, were called rappers. They might go on for years, then suddenly stop, but no one who had heard the noise, with its suggestion of furious physical frustration, as though whatever was behind it could not get out, was ever likely to mistake it for anything else. 'Your rapper's been at my adjustable spanners,' said the plumber, without rancour, when she came to see how the work was going forward. His tool bag had been upended and scattered; pale blue tiles with a nice design of waterlilies had been flung broadside about the upstairs passage. The bathroom, with its water supply half connected, had the alert air of having witnessed something. When the well-disposed plumber had gone to his tea, she shut the bathroom door, waited a few moments, and then looked sharply in again. Anyone watching her, she reflected, might have thought she was mad. The word in Hardborough for 'mad' was 'not quite right', just as 'very ill' was 'moderate'. 'Perhaps I'll end up not quite right if this goes on,' she told the plumber, wishing he wouldn't call it 'your rapper'. The plumber, Mr Wilkins, thought that she would weather it.

It was on occasions like this that she particularly missed the good friends of her early days at Müller's. When she had come in and taken off her suede glove to show her engagement ring, a diamond chip, there had been a hearteningly long list of names on the subscription list for her present, and it was almost the same list when Charlie had died of pneumonia in an improvised reception camp at the beginning of the war. Nearly all the girls in Mailing, Despatch and Counter Staff had lost touch; and even when she had their addresses, she found herself unwilling to admit that they had grown as old as she had.

It was not that she was short of acquaintances in Hardborough. At Rhoda's Dressmaker's, for example, she was well liked. But her confidence was hardly respected. Rhoda – that is to say, Jessie Welford – who had been asked to make her up a new dress, did not hesitate to speak about it freely, and even to show the material.

'It's for General and Mrs Gamart's party at The Stead. I don't know that I'd've chosen red myself. They've guests coming down from London.'

Florence, although she knew Mrs Gamart to nod to, and to be smiled at by, after various collections for charity, had never expected to be invited to The Stead. She took it, even though none of her stock had arrived as yet from London, as a compliment to the power of books themselves.

As soon as Sam Wilkins had fixed the bath to his own satisfaction, and the tiles were re-pegged on the roof, Florence Green moved out of her flat and boldly took up residence, with her few things, at the Old House. Even with the waterlily tiles firmly hung, it was not an altogether reassuring place to live. The curious sounds associated with the haunting continued at night, long after the ill-connected water pipes had fallen silent. But courage and endurance are useless if they are never tested. She only hoped that there would be no interruption when Jessie Welford brought the new dress in for a fitting. But this particular ordeal never arose. A message came, asking her to try on at Rhoda's, next door.

'I think perhaps it's not my colour after all. Would you call it ruby?' It was a comfort when Jessie said that it was more like a garnet, or a deep rust. But there was something unsatisfactory in the red, or rust, reflexion which seemed to move unwillingly in the looking-glass.

'It doesn't seem to fit at all at the back. Perhaps if I try to stand against the wall most of the time . . .'

'It'll come to you as you wear it,' the dressmaker replied firmly. 'You need a bit of costume jewellery as a focus.'

'Are you sure?' asked Florence. The fitting seemed to be turning into a conspiracy to prevent anyone noticing her new dress at all.

'I dare say, when all's said and done, I'm more used to dressing up and going out in the evening than you are,' said Miss Welford. 'I'm a bridge player, you know. Not much doing here – I go over to Flintmarket twice a week. A penny a hundred in the mornings, and twopence a hundred in the evenings. We wear long skirts then, of course.'

She walked backwards a couple of steps, throwing a shadow over the glass, then returned to pin and adjust. No change, Florence knew, would make her look anything but small.

'I wish I wasn't going to this party,' she said.

'Well, I wouldn't mind taking your place. It's a pity Mrs Gamart sees fit to order everything from London, but it will be properly done – no need to stand and count the sandwiches. And when you get there, you won't have to bother about how you look. Nobody will mind you, and anyway you'll find you know everyone in the room.'

Florence had felt sure she would not, and she did not. The Stead, in any case, was not the kind of place where hats and coats were left about in the hall so that you could guess, before committing yourself to an entrance, who was already there. The hall, boarded with polished elm, breathed the deep warmth of a house that has never been cold. She caught a glimpse of herself in a glass much more brilliant that Rhoda's, and wished that she had not worn red.

Through the door ahead unfamiliar voices could be heard from a beautiful room, painted in the pale green which at that time the Georgian Society still recommended. Silver photograph frames on the piano and on small tables permitted a glimpse of the network of family relations which gave Violet Gamart an access to power far beyond Hardborough itself. Her husband, the General, was opening drawers and cupboards with the object of not finding anything, to give him an excuse to wander from room to room. In the 1950s there were many plays on the London stage where the characters made frequent entrances and exits out of various doors and were seen again in the second act, three hours later. The General would have fitted well into such a play. He hovered, alert and experimentally smiling, among the refreshments, hoping that he would soon be needed, even if only for a few moments, since opening champagne is not woman's work.

There was no bank manager there, no Vicar, not even Mr Thornton, Florence's solicitor, or Mr Drury, the solicitor who was not her solicitor. She recognized the back of the rural dean, and that was all. It was a party for the county, and for visitors from London. She correctly guessed that she would find out in time why she herself had been asked.

The General, relieved to see a smallish woman who did not appear to be intimidating or a relation of his wife's, gave her a large glass of champagne from one of the dozen he had opened. If she was not a relation of his wife's there were no elementary blunders to be made, but although he felt certain he had seen her somewhere before, God knew who she was exactly. She followed his thoughts, which, indeed, were transparent in their dogged progress from one difficulty to another, and told him that she was the person who was going to open a bookshop.

'That's it, of course. Got it in one. You're thinking of opening a bookshop. Violet was interested in it. She wanted to have one or two of those words of hers with you about it. I expect she'll have a chance later.'

Since Mrs Gamart was the hostess, she could have had this chance at any time, but Florence did not deceive herself about her own importance. She drank some of the champagne, and the smaller worries of the day seemed to stream upwards as tiny pinpricks through the golden mouthfuls and to break harmlessly and vanish.

She had expected the General to feel that his duty was discharged, but he lingered.

'What kind of stuff are you going to have in your shop?' he asked.

She scarcely knew how to answer him.

'They don't have many books of poetry these days, do they?' he persisted. 'I don't see many of them about.'

'I shall have some poetry, of course. It doesn't sell quite as well as some other things. But it will take time to get to know all the stock.'

The General looked surprised. It had never taken him a long time, as a subaltern, to get to know all his men.

'"It is easy to be dead. Say only this, they are dead." Do you know who wrote that?'

She would dearly have liked to have been able to say yes, but couldn't. The faltering light of expectancy in the General's eyes died down. Clearly he had tried to make this point before, perhaps many times. In a voice so low that against the noise of the party that sipped and clattered round them she could only just hear it, he went on:

'Charles Sorley . . .'

She realized at once that Sorley must be dead.

'How old was he?'

'Sorley? He was twenty. He was in the Swedebashers – the Suffolks, you know – 9th Battalion, B Company. He was killed in the battle of Loos, in 1915. He'd have been sixty-four years old if he'd lived. I'm sixty-four myself. That makes me think of poor Sorley.'

The General shuffled away into the mounting racket. Florence was alone, surrounded by people who spoke to each other familiarly, and some of whom could be seen in replica in the silver frames. Who were they all? She didn't mind; for, after all, they would have felt lost in their turn if they had found their way into the Mailing Department at Müller's. A mild young man's voice said from just behind her, 'I know who you are. You must be Mrs Green.'

He wouldn't say that, she thought, unless he was sure of being recognized himself, and she did recognize him. Everybody in Hardborough could have told you who he was, in a sense proudly, because he was known to drive up to London to work, and to be something in TV. He was Milo North, from Nelson Cottage, on the corner of Back Lane. Exactly what he did was uncertain, but Hardborough was used to not being quite certain what people did in London.

Milo North was tall, and went through life with singularly little effort. To say 'I know who you are, you must be Mrs Green' represented an unaccustomed output of energy. What seemed delicacy in him was usually a way of avoiding trouble; what seemed like sympathy was the instinct to prevent trouble before it started. It was hard to see what growing older would mean to such a person. His emotions, from lack of exercise, had disappeared almost altogether. Adaptability and curiosity, he had found, did just as well.

'I know who you are, of course, Mr North,' she said, 'but I've never had an invitation to The Stead before. I expect you come here often.'

'I'm asked here often,' said Milo. He gave her another glass of champagne, and having expected to be left indefinitely by herself after the retreat of the General, she was grateful.

'You're very kind.'

'Not very,' said Milo, who rarely said anything that was not true. Gentleness is not kindness. His fluid personality tested and stole into the weak places of others until it found it could settle down to its own advantage. 'You live by yourself, don't you? You've just moved into the Old House all by yourself? Haven't you ever thought of marrying again?'

Florence felt confused. It seemed to her that she was becalmed with this young man in some backwater, while louder voices grew more incoherent beyond. Time seemed to move faster there. Plates that had been full of sandwiches and crowned with parsley when she came in now held nothing but crumbs.

'I was very happily married, since you ask,' she said. 'My husband used to work in the same place as I did. Then he went into the old Board of Trade, before it became a Ministry. He used to tell me about his work when he came home in the evenings.'

'And you were happy?'

'I loved him, and I tried to understand his work. It sometimes strikes me that men and women aren't quite the right people for each other. Something must be, of course.'

Milo looked at her more closely.

'Are you sure you're well advised to undertake the running of a business?' he asked.

'I've never met you before, Mr North, but I've felt that because of your work you might welcome a bookshop in Hardborough. You must meet writers at the BBC, and thinkers, and so forth. I expect they come down here sometimes to see you, and to get some fresh air.'

'If they did I shouldn't quite know what to do with them. Writers will go anywhere, I'm not sure about thinkers. Kattie would look after them, I expect, though.'

Kattie must certainly be the dark girl in red stockings – or perhaps they were tights, which were now obtainable in

23

Lowestoft and Flintmarket, though not in Hardborough – who lived with Milo North. They were the only unmarried couple living together in the town. But Kattie, who was also known to work for the BBC, only came down three nights a week, on Mondays, Wednesdays, and Fridays, which was thought to make it a little more respectable.

'It's a pity that Kattie couldn't be here tonight.'

'But it's Wednesday!' Mrs Green exclaimed, in spite of herself.

'I didn't say she wasn't down here, only that it was a pity that she couldn't come. She couldn't come because I didn't bring her. I thought it might cause more trouble than it was worth.'

Mrs Green thought that he ought to have had the courage of his convictions. Her notion was of a young couple defying the world. She herself was older, and had the right to anxiety.

'At any rate, you must come to my shop,' she said. 'I shall rely on you.'

'On no account,' Milo replied.

He took her by both elbows, the lightest possible touch, and shook her by way of emphasis.

'Why are you wearing red this evening?' he asked.

'It isn't red! It's garnet, or deep rust!'

Mrs Violet Gamart, the natural patroness of all public activities in Hardborough, came towards them. Although her back had been turned, she had noticed the shake but felt that it was suggestive of the freedom of the arts and therefore not out of place in her drawing-room. The moment, however, had come for her to have a few words with Mrs Green. She explained that she had been attempting to do this all evening, but had been repeatedly spirited away. So many people seemed to have come, but most of them she could see at any time. What she really wanted to say was how grateful everyone must feel about this new venture, such foresight and enterprise.

Mrs Gamart spoke with a kind of generous urgency. She had dark bright eyes which appeared to be kept open, as though by some mechanism, to their widest extent.

'Bruno! Have you been introduced to my husband? Come and tell Mrs – Mrs – how delighted we all are.'

Florence felt a muddled sense of vocation, as though she would willingly devote her life to the service of Mrs Gamart.

'Bruno!'

The General had been trying to call attention to an abrasion on his hand, caused by the twisted wire on one of the champagne corks. He went up to every group of guests in turn, hoping to raise a smile by referring to himself as walking wounded.

'We've all be praying for a good bookshop in Hardborough, haven't we, Bruno?'

Glad to be summoned, he halted towards her.

'Of course, my dear, no harm in praying. Probably be a good thing if we all did more of it.'

'There's only one point, Mrs Green, a small one in a way – you haven't actually moved into the Old House yet, have you?'

'Yes, I've been there for more than a week.'

'Oh, but there's no water.'

'Sam Wilkins connected the pipes for me.'

'Don't forget, Violet,' the General said anxiously, 'that you've been up in London a good deal lately, and haven't been able to keep an eye on everything.'

'Why shouldn't I have moved in?' Florence asked, as lightly as she could manage.

'You mustn't laugh at me, but I'm fortunate enough to have a kind of gift, or perhaps it's an instinct, of fitting people and places together. For instance, only just recently – only I'm afraid it wouldn't mean very much to you if you don't know the two houses I'm talking about – '

'Perhaps you could tell me which ones you're thinking of,'

said the General, 'and then I could explain it all slowly to Mrs Green.'

'Anyway, to return to the Old House – that's exactly the sort of thing I mean. I believe I might be able to save you a great deal of disappointment, and even perhaps a certain amount of expense. In fact, I want to help you, and that's my excuse for saying all this.'

'I am sure no excuse is needed,' said Florence.

'There are so many more suitable premises in Hardborough, so much more convenient in every way for a bookshop. Did you know, for example, that Deben is closing down?'

Certainly she knew that Deben's wet fish shop was about to close. Everybody in the town knew when there were likely to be vacant premises, who was in financial straits, who would need larger family accommodation in nine months, and who was about to die.

'We've been so used, I'm afraid, to the Old House standing empty that we've delayed from year to year – you've quite put us to shame by being in such a hurry, Mrs Green – but the fact is that we're rather upset by the sudden transformation of our Old House into a shop – so many of us have the idea of converting it into some kind of centre – I mean an arts centre – for Hardborough.'

The General was listening with strained attention.

'Might pray for that too, you know, Violet.'

'. . . chamber music in summer – we can't leave it all to Aldeburgh – lecturers in winter . . .'

'We have lectures already,' said Florence. 'The Vicar's series on Picturesque Suffolk only comes round again every three years.' They were delightful evenings, for there was no need to listen closely, and in front of the slumberous rows the coloured slides followed each other in no sort of order, disobedient to the Vicar's voice.

'We should have to be a good deal more ambitious, particularly with the summer visitors who may come from some distance away. And there is simply no other old house that would give the right ambience. Do, won't you, think it over?'

'I've been negotiating this sale for more than six months, and I can't believe that everyone in Hardborough didn't know about it. In fact, I'm sure they did.' She looked for confirmation to the General, who stared fixedly away at the empty sandwich plates.

'And of course,' Mrs Gamart went on, with even more marked emphasis, 'one great advantage, which it seems almost wrong to throw away, is that now we have exactly the right person to take charge. I mean to take charge of the centre, and put us all right about books and pictures and music, and encourage things, and get things off the ground, and keep things going, and see they're on the right lines.'

She gave Mrs Green a smile of unmistakable meaning and radiance. The moment of confusing intimacy had returned, even though Mrs Gamart, in the course of her last sentence, had withdrawn, with encouraging nods and gestures, into her protective horde of guests.

Florence, left quite alone, went out to the small room off the hall to begin the search for her coat. While she looked methodically through the piles, she reflected that, after all, she was not too old to do two jobs, perhaps get a manager for the bookshop, while she herself would have to take some sort of course in art history and music appreciation – music was always appreciated, whereas art had a history – that, she supposed, would mean journeys over to Cambridge.

Outside it was a clear night and she could see across the marshes to the Laze, marked by the riding lights of the fishing boats, waiting for the low tide. But it was cold, and the air stung her face.

'It was very good of them to ask me,' she thought. 'I daresay they found me a bit awkward to talk to.'

As soon as she had gone, the groups of guests re-formed

themselves, as the cattle had done when Raven took the old horse aside. Now they were all of the same kind, facing one way, grazing together. Between themselves they could arrange many matters, though what they arranged was quite often a matter of chance. As the time drew on for thinking about going home, Mrs Gamart was still a little disturbed as what seemed a check in her scheme for the Old House. This Mrs Green, though unobtrusive enough, had not quite agreed to everything on the spot. It was not of much importance. But a little more champagne, given her by Milo, caused her mind to revolve in its giddy uppermost circle, and to her cousin's second husband, who was something to do with the Arts Council, and to her own cousin once removed, who was soon going to be high up in the Directorate of Planning, and to her brilliant nephew who sat for the Longwash Division of West Suffolk and had already made his name as the persevering secretary of the Society for Providing Public Access to Places of Interest and Beauty, and to Lord Gosfield who had ventured over from his stagnant castle in the Fens because if foot-and-mouth broke out again he wouldn't be able to come for months, she spoke of the Hardborough Centre for Music and the Arts. And in the minds of her brilliant nephew, cousin, and so on, a faint resolution formed that something might have to be done, or Violet might become rather a nuisance. Even Lord Gosfield was touched, though he had said nothing all evening, and had in fact driven the hundred odd miles expressly to say nothing in the company of his old friend Bruno. They were all kind to their hostess, because it made life easier.

It was time to be gone. They were not sure where they or their wives had put the car keys. They lingered at the front door saying that they must not let in the cold air, while the General's old dog, which lived in single-minded expectation of the door opening, thumped its tail feebly on the shining floor; then their cars would not start and the prospect of some of them returning to stay the night grew perilously close; then the last spark ignited and they roared away, calling and waving, and the marsh wind could be heard again in the silence that followed.

3

The next morning Florence prepared herself a herring –
there was not much point in living in East Suffolk if one
didn't know how to do this – two slices of bread and butter,
and a pot of tea. Her cooker was in the backhouse. This was
the most companionable room in the Old House, white-
washed, with not much noise beyond the sighing of the old
bricked-up well in the floor. Previous residents had counted
themselves lucky that they did not have to go outdoors to
pump, luckier still when the great buff-glazed sink, deep as a
sarcophagus, was installed. A brass tap, proudly flared,
discharged ice-cold water from a great height.

At eight o'clock she unplugged her electric kettle and
plugged in her radio set, which immediately began to speak
of trouble in Cyprus and Nyasaland and then told her, with
a slight change of intonation, that the expectation of life was
now 68.1 years for males and 73.9 years for females, as
opposed to 45.8 for males and 52.4 for females at the
beginning of the century. She tried to feel that this was
encouraging. But the Warning To Shipping – North Sea,
wind cyclonic variable strong becoming NE strong or gale
sea rough or very rough – moved her to shame. She was
ashamed of sitting in her backhouse and of her herring from
the deep, and of the uselessness of feeling ashamed. Through
her east-facing window she could see the storm warning
hauled up over the Coastguards against a sky that was pale
yellowish green.

By mid-day it was clear. The sky brightened from one
horizon to the other, and the high white cloud was reflected

in mile after mile of shining dyke water, so that the marshes seemed to stand between cloud and cloud. After her morning errands she took a short-cut back across the common. The Primary School were having their second play out. Boys separated from girls, except for the top class, coming up to their eleven plus, who circled round each other. Entirely alone, a small child stood howling. It had been well sent out, with a scarf crossed over the chest and secured behind with a safety-pin, and woollen gloves fastened to a length of elastic passed round under the coat collar. Patently it was a Mixed Infant, unqualified to mingle with either boys or girls. She attempted to calm it.

'You're from the Infants, you oughtn't to be playing out now. Are you lost? What's your name?'

'Melody Gipping.'

Florence took out a clean handkerchief and blew Melody's nose. A waif-like figure, with hair as fine as dry grass, detached itself from the Girls.

'That's all right, miss. I'm Christine Gipping, I'll take her. We've got Kleenex at ours – they're more hygienic.'

The two of them strayed back together. The Boys were shooting each other dead, the Girls bounced old tennis balls, forming a wide ring, and sang.

> One, two, Pepsi-Cola,
> Three, four, Casanova,
> Five, six, hair in rollers,
> Seven, eight, roll her over,
> Nine, ten, do it again.

Florence looked southwards, where the horizon was bounded by a dark stretch of pine woods. That was the Heronry, but in 1953, when the sea had drowned the woodlands in salt, the herons had flown away and no longer nested there.

At the kissing-gate which led off the common, she saw

31

approaching her, stalking her almost, with the sideways look of the failed tradesman, Mr Deben from the wet fish shop. He must have followed her up there, indeed he as good as admitted it.

'It's about my place, Mrs Green. It's going up for auction, but that won't be till April, or it might be later still. I'd very much prefer to come to terms privately before that. Now, as you've expressed an interest in the property – ' He did not pause long enough for her to say that she had done nothing of the kind, but hurried on: 'If you're not going to remain at the Old House, and if you're not leaving the district altogether – you'll appreciate I'm too busy to pay attention to all the rumours I hear – well then, it stands to reason you'll have to make an offer for another place.'

He must be distracted by his business worries, she thought. He had come straight out of his shop with his fishmonger's straw hat still on his head, and a dreadful old suit of overalls. Meanwhile his sly and muddled discourse had brought an idea to her mind, sudden but not strange, for she recognized it immediately as the truth. It was the truth in the form of a warning, for which she must be thankful.

'There has been a misunderstanding, Mr Deben. But that doesn't matter in the least, and I should like to help you. Mrs Gamart was kind enough to tell me about her scheme for an arts centre – which would, I'm sure, benefit every one of us here in Hardborough. She is, I believe, looking about for premises, and what could be better than a vacant wet fish shop?'

Without giving herself time for reflection, she left the common by the kissing-gate, which stuck awkwardly, as usual, while she and Deben exchanged politenesses, crossed the High Street, turned right by the Corn and Seed Merchant's, and right again for Nelson Cottage. Milo North could be seen through the downstairs window, sitting at a table with a patchwork cloth, and doing absolutely nothing.

'Why aren't you up in London?' she asked, rapping on the pane. She felt mildly irritated by the unpredictability of his daily life.

'I've sent Kattie to work this morning. Do come in.'

Milo opened the tiny front door. He was much too tall for the house, which was tarred and painted black, like the fishermen's huts.

'Perhaps you'd like some Nescafé?'

'I have never had any,' she said. 'I have heard of it. I'm told it's not prepared with boiling water.' She sat down in a delicate bentwood rocking-chair. 'These things are all much too small for you,' she said.

'I know, I know. I'm glad you came this morning. Nobody else ever makes me face the truth.'

'That's fortunate, because I came to ask you a question. When Mrs Gamart was talking at her party about the ideal person to run an arts centre, it was you, of course, wasn't it, that she had in mind?'

'Violet's party?'

'She expected me to move out – probably, in fact, to move somewhere else altogether – with the understanding that you would come to the Old House to manage everything?'

Milo gazed at her with limpid grey eyes. 'If she meant me, I don't think she could have used the word "manage".'

Florence accused herself of vanity, self-deception, and wilful misconstruction. She was a tradeswoman: why should anyone expect her to have anything to do with the arts? Curiously enough, for the next few days she was on the verge of offering to leave the Old House. The suspicion that she was clinging on simply because her vanity had been wounded was unbearable. – Of course, Mrs Gamart, whom I shall never speak of or refer to as Violet, it was Milo North you had in mind. Instal him immediately. My little book business can be fitted in anywhere. I only ask you not to allow the conventions to be defied too rapidly – East Suffolk isn't used to it. Kattie will have to live, for the first few years at least, in the oyster warehouse.

In calmer moments she reflected that if Mrs Gamart and her supporters could extract some kind of Government grant and could afford to pay her price for the freehold, plus moving expenses and a fair profit, she would be open to new opportunities, perhaps not in Suffolk, or even in England, and with that precious sense of beginning again which she could not expect too often at her age. No doubt it was absurd to imagine that she was being driven out, and that the hand of privilege was impelling her to Deben's wet fish shop.

She blinded herself, in short, by pretending for a while that human beings are not divided into exterminators and exterminatees, with the former, at any given moment, predominating. Will-power is useless without a sense of direction. Hers was at such a low ebb that it no longer gave her the instructions for survival.

It revived, however, without any effort on her part, and within the space of ten minutes on a Tuesday morning at the end of March. The weather was curious, and reminded her of the day she saw the flying heron trying to swallow the eel. While the washing on the lines was blowing to the west with the inshore breeze, the pumping mill on the marshes had caught the land breeze and was turning east. The rooks circled in the warring currents of the air. She left her little car in the garage next to the Coastguards, which was as near as she could manage to the Old House, and took the short lane or passageway from the foreshore which led to her backhouse door.

The passage was very narrow, and in a hard blow the little brick-and-tile houses seemed to cling to each other, as the saying went, like a sailor's child. Her back door had to

34

—

be opened carefully, or the draught blew out the pilot light in the cooker. She turned the key in the mortice lock, but the door would not open.

She wasted only a moment's thought on stiff hinges, warped wood, and so on. The hostile force, pushing against her push, came and went, always a little ahead of her, with the shrewdness of the insane. The quivering door waited for her to try again. From inside the backhouse came a burst of tapping. It did not sound like one thing hitting another, more like a series of tiny explosions. Then, as she leaned against her door, trying to recover her breath, it suddenly collapsed violently, swinging to and fro, like a hand clapping a comic spectacle, as she fell inwards on to the brick floor on her knees.

Everyone in Score Lane must have seen her pitch head foremost into her own kitchen. But stronger than the embarrassment, fear and pain was the sense of injustice. The rapper was a familiar of the bathroom and the upstairs passage. In the backhouse she had never heard or seen any signs of malignancy. There are unspoken agreements even with the metaphysical, and the rapper had overstepped them. Her will-power, which she felt as indignation, rose to meet the injury. The Unseen, as the girls had always called it at Müller's, could mind its own business no better than the Seen. Neither of them would prevent her from opening a bookshop.

In consequence, Mr Thornton was instructed to finalize the business as soon as possible, which meant that he proceeded at the same pace as before. Thornton & Co had been established for many years. The court work might be largely left to Drury, the solicitor who wasn't Thornton, but Thornton was reliable through and through. He had heard, of course, that his client had been seen falling about the street, holding a horse's head for that old scoundrel Raven, and calling on Milo North, of whom Thornton disapproved.

35

On the other hand, she had been asked to a party at The Stead, where he himself had never been invited, although he still hoped that the Gamarts would see sense one day and transfer their affairs from Drury, who was simply not up to handling important family business. Well, so Mrs Green knew the Gamarts. But even about that, he believed, there were reservations.

Taking out his file on the Old House, he explained that there was some little difficulty about the oyster warehouse. It could be upheld that the fishing community, by right immemorial, were entitled to walk straight through it on their way to the shore, and possibly to dry their sails in the loft.

'You don't get to the shore if you walk through the warehouse,' she pointed out. 'You get to the gas-manager's office. Nothing can be dried there anyway – the walls are running with condensation. The loft has fallen to pieces, and none of the longshore fishermen go out under sail. Surely that question won't take long to settle.'

The solicitor explained that rights were in no way affected by the impossibility of putting them into practice. Conveyancing, he added, was not as simple as the general public imagined. 'I'm pleased that you called in today, as a matter of fact, Mrs Green. Something that I heard, quite by chance, made me wonder whether you were thinking better of the whole transaction.' He appeared to be trembling with curiosity.

'By thinking better you mean thinking worse, of course,' she said.

'Having second thoughts, dear lady. It's always sad to think of losing a member of a small community like Hardborough, but if there are greater opportunities elsewhere, one can only applaud and understand.'

'You mean you thought I might want to change my mind and go somewhere else?' She wished that she could grow much taller, if only for half an hour, so that she could look down, rather than up, during interviews like these. 'You mean you thought I wanted to get out of the Old House – which, by the way, is my only home – while you're still dithering about the fishermen's right of way?'

'There are many other empty properties in Hardborough, and, as it happens, I have a list of some other ones farther afield – Flintmarket, and even Ipswich. I don't know whether you've considered . . .'

It was May, and flocks of terns had arrived, rising and falling with every wingbeat, and settling by the hundred on the sandy patches towards the shore. The stock from Müller's came down in two Carter Paterson vans, followed a week later by orders from the book wholesalers. For the rest, for the new titles, she would have to wait for the salesmen, if they would venture so far across the marshes to a completely unknown point of sale. Since the warehouse had proved unusable, everything had to be piled into the spacious cupboard under the stairs while Florence pondered the arrangement.

She drove back one morning from Flintmarket to find the premises full of twelve- and thirteen-year-old boys in blue jerseys. They were Sea Scouts, they told her.

'How did you get in?'

'Mr Raven got the key from the plumber,' said one of the children, square and reliable as a straw-bale.

'He's not your skipper, is he?'

'No, but he told us to come over to yours. What do you want doing?'

'I want all the shelves put up,' she said, with equal directness. 'Can you do that?'

'How many hand-drills can you get us, miss?'

She went out and bought hand-drills, and screws by the pound. The scouts worked for two hours, went home for

37

their dinners, and then knocked on again. By the time the shelves were up, the whole floor, and most of the books, were covered with a quarter-inch layer of sawdust.

'We could make it good later, and clear up this lot,' Wally said.

'I shall clear up myself,' she said. She felt overwhelmed with love for them. 'I'd like to give you something for your headquarters.' Scout Headquarters was the wreck of an old three-masted schooner, beached on the estuary.

'Have you got any morse codes, or *Pears Medical Dictionary*?'

'I'm afraid not.' They were both at a loss. 'I tell you what, Wally. I want you to take these hand-drills. They're no use to me, I don't know how to use them properly. If I want a hole made in anything, I shall have to send you a signal.'

'Thank you. I daresay we could make use of those,' said Wally, 'but with every job we undertake we're obliged to contribute the value of twelve bricks to the new Baden-Powell House that they're building up in South Kensington.'

She gave him five pounds, and he saluted.

'South Kensington's an area of London,' he explained.

The scouts, over whom Raven exerted a mysterious but direct influence, returned to do the white-painting, and then she was free, refusing any further offers, to arrange the stock herself.

New books came in sets of eighteen, wrapped in thin brown paper. As she sorted them out, they fell into their own social hierarchy. The heavy luxurious country-house books, the books about Suffolk churches, the memoirs of statesmen in several volumes, took the place that was theirs by right of birth in the front window. Others, indispensable, but not aristocratic, would occupy the middle shelves. That was the place for the Books of the Car – from Austin to Wolseley – technical works on pebble-polishing, sailing, pony clubs, wild flowers and birds, local maps and guide books. Among these the popular war reminiscences, in jackets of khaki and blood-red, faced each other as rivals with bristling hostility. Back in the shadows went the Stickers, largely philosophy and poetry, which she had little hope of ever seeing the last of. The Stayers – dictionaries, reference books and so forth – would go straight to the back, with the Bibles and reward books which, it was hoped, Mrs Traill of the Primary would present to successful pupils. Last of all came the crates of Müller's shabby remainders. A few were even second-hand. Although she had been trained never to look inside the books while at work, she opened one or two of them – old Everyman editions in faded olive boards stamped with gold. There was the elaborate endpaper which she had puzzled over when she was a little girl. *A good book is the precious lifeblood of a master spirit, embalmed and treasured up on purpose to a life beyond life.* After some hesitation, she put it between Religion and Home Medicine.

The right-hand wall she kept for paperbacks. At 1s. 6d. each, cheerfully coloured, brightly democratic, they crowded the shelves in well-disciplined ranks. They would have a rapid turnover and she had to approve of them; yet she could remember a world where only foreigners had been content to have their books bound in paper. The Everymans, in their shabby dignity, seemed to confront them with a look of reproach.

In the backhouse kitchen, since there was absolutely no room for them in the shop itself, were two deep drawers set apart for the Books of the Books – the Ledger, Repeat Orders, Purchases, Sales Returns, Petty Cash. Still blank, with untouched double columns, these unloved books menaced the silent commonwealth on the shelves next door. Not much of a hand at accounts, Florence would have preferred them to remain without readers. This was weakness, and she asked Jessie Welford's sharp niece, who worked with a firm of accountants in Lowestoft, to come over once a month for a check. 'A little Trial Balance now and then,' said Ivy

Welford condescendingly, as though it were a tonic for the feeble-minded. Her worldly wisdom, in a girl of twenty-one, was alarming, and she would need paying, of course; but both Mr Thornton and the bank manager seemed relieved when they heard that Ivy had been arranged for. Her head was well screwed-on, they said.

4

The Old House Bookshop was to open next morning, but Florence did not have it in mind to hold any kind of celebration, because she was uncertain who should be asked. The frame of mind, however, is everything. Given that, one can have a very satisfactory party all by oneself. She was thinking this when the street door opened and Raven came in.

'You're often alone,' he remarked.

He apologized for wearing his waders, and looked round to see what kind of a job the scouts had made of the shelving.

'An eighth of an inch out over there by the cupboard.'

But she would have no fault found. Besides, now that the books were in place, well to the front (she couldn't bear them to slide back as though defeated), any irregularities could scarcely be noticed. Like the red dress, the shelving would come to her as she wore it.

'And that plastering looks unsightly,' Raven went on. 'You can point that out, next time you see them.'

She did not feel confident that she would recognize any of the scouts out of uniform; but she was wrong, for Wally appeared, dressed in his school blazer and a serviceable pair of trousers from the Agricultural Outfitters, and she knew him at once.

He had a message, he said, for Mrs Green.

'Who gave it you?' Raven asked.

'Mr Brundish did, Mr Raven.'

'What? He came out of Holt House and gave it to you?'

'No, he just leaned a bit against the window and clicked.'

41

'With his tongue?'

'No, with his fingers.'

'Then you couldn't hear it through the window?'

'No, it was more like I was aware of it.'

'How did he look, then? Palish?'

Wally seemed doubtful. 'Palish and darkish. You can't really say how he looks. His head's a bit sunk down between his shoulders.'

'Were you scared?'

'I felt I'd have to jump to it.'

'A Sea Scout should always jump to it,' Raven replied automatically. 'I don't reckon to have seen him for more than a month, in spite of the fine weather, and I haven't heard him speak for much longer. He didn't say anything to you, did he?'

'Oh yes, he cleared his throat a bit, and told me to give this to Mrs Green.'

Wally had in his hand a white envelope bordered with black. Although she had been staring at it all this time, she took it almost with disbelief. She had never spoken to Mr Brundish. Even at the party at The Stead she had had no expectation of meeting him. It was well known that Mrs Gamart, as patroness of all that was of value in Hardborough, would have liked to count him as a friend, but since she had been at The Stead for only fifteen years and was not of Suffolk origin, her wishes had been in vain. Perhaps her presence had not been drawn to Mr Brundish's attention. And then, of recent years he had been so much confined to his home that it was a matter of astonishment that he should know her name.

'I don't see how this can be for me.'

It did not occur to either Raven or Wally to go away until she had opened it.

'Don't you worry about the black edges,' Raven said. 'He had those envelopes done it must have been in 1919, when they all came back from the first war, and I was still a nipper, and Mrs Brundish died.'

'What did she die of?'

'That was an odd thing, Mrs Green. She was drowned crossing the marshes.'

Inside the envelope was one sheet of paper, also black-bordered.

Dear Madam,

I should like to wish you well. In my great-grandfather's time there was a bookseller in the High Street who, I believe, knocked down one of the customers with a folio when he grew too quarrelsome. There had been some delay in the arrival of the latest instalment of a new novel – I think, *Dombey and Son*. From that day to this, no one has been courageous enough to sell books in Hardborough. You are doing us an honour. I should certainly visit your shop if I ever went out, but nowadays I make a point of not doing so; however, I shall be very willing to subscribe to your circulating library.

Yours obediently,

Edmund Brundish.

A library! She hadn't contemplated it, and there was nothing like enough room.

'He's evidently not satisfied with the Mobile,' said Raven.

The public library van came over from Flintmarket once a month. The books, from much use, had acquired a peculiar fragrance. All who cared for reading in Hardborough had read them several times.

She accompanied Wally, who nodded acknowledgment to her thanks, to the street door. He appeared to be a general messenger. His bike was loaded with shopping, and from the handlebars, which he had screwed on upside down to look more like a racer, hung a wicker basket containing a hen.

'She's broody, Mrs Green. I'm taking her round from ours to my cousin's half-sister's. She wants to rear chicks.'

Florence put her hand lightly on the slumbering mass of feathers. The old fowl was sunk into a soft tawny heap, scarcely opening her slit-like eyes. Her whole energy was absorbed in producing warmth. The basket itself throbbed with a slow and purposeful rhythm.

'Thank you for bringing the note, Wally. I can see you've got plenty to do.' She had brought her bag, and subscribed quietly to another brick.

Raven did not leave at once. He explained that he had come in the first instance to suggest that she needed a bright youngster to give her a hand, perhaps after school.

'Were you thinking of Wally?'

'No, not him. He won't be at home with books. It's maths that attracts him. If he'd been much of a reader, he'd have taken a look at your letter on the way over here, and you could see he hadn't done that.'

Raven was thinking of one of the Gipping girls. He didn't say how many of them there were, or appear to think that it mattered which one. The reputation for competence was shed upon them by their mother, Mrs Gipping. The family lived in that house between the church and the old railway station, with a fair piece of ground. Mr Gipping was a plasterer but could be glimpsed often from the rear staking peas or earthing up his potatoes. Mrs Gipping went out to work a little. She favoured Milo, on the days when Kattie was up in London, and she went regularly to Mr Brundish.

'I'll speak to her,' Raven said. 'She can send one of her lot down after school. That finishes at twenty-five past three.'

He took his leave. The wet footprints of his waders looked like the track of some friendly amphibian across the floor-boards, polished more than once for tomorrow's opening. The sensation of having something organized for her was

44

agreeable. Left to herself, she would not have had the confidence to call at Mrs Gipping's populous house.

Her mind went back reluctantly to the problem of the lending library. It would be a nuisance, and might even be a failure. Could Mrs Gamart, for instance, reasonably be expected to subscribe to it? Nothing more had been heard from The Stead, but Deben had given a half-reproachful, half-knowing glance as he laid out the sprats on his marble slab, which had shown her that the controversy was still alive. The more modestly she ran her business, for the first year at least, the better. But after reading Mr Brundish's letter through again, she said aloud, 'I will see what I can do about a library.'

If she had thought that the poltergeist would relax its efforts after the shop had opened, she was wrong. At various times in the night, behind every screw which the scouts had driven in, there would be a delicate sharp tap, as though they were being numbered for future reference. The customers, during the day, would remark that it was very noisy at Rhoda's next door, and that they had never heard a sewing-machine make a noise like that before. Florence would reply, conscious of telling the exact truth, that you could never tell with these old houses. She installed a cash register with a bell, a sound that will distract the attention from almost anything else.

Her opening day had drawn only mild attention in Hardborough. There was no curiosity about the Old House itself. It had stood empty so long, with broken windows and unlocked doors, that every child in the district had played there. The turnover for the first week had been between £70 and £80. Mrs Traill from the Primary had made a clearance of *Daily Life in Ancient Britain*, Mr Thornton bought a birdwatching book and the bank manager, rather unexpectedly, one on physical fitness. Mr Drury, the solicitor who was not Mr Thornton, and one of the doctors from Surgery,

45

both bought books by former SAS men, who had been parachuted into Europe and greatly influenced the course of the war; they also placed orders for books by Allied commanders who poured scorn on the SAS men, and questioned their credentials. That was on Tuesday. On Wednesday, when rain set in, the local girls' boarding school, out for a walk, had taken refuge in the shop, which was entirely filled, like a sheep-pen, with damp bodies closely pressed toegther and gently steaming. The girls turned over the greeting-cards, which had been grudgingly given a space next to the paperbacks, and bought three. Envelopes had to be found, and the till stuck when it was called upon to add 9½d., 6½d., and 3½d. On Thursday – which was early closing, but Florence decided to make her first week an exception – Deben appeared, to show that there were no hard feelings, and poked round, running his scrubbed hands over the fitments. He asked for a vocal score of the *Messiah*.

'Do you want me to put that on order?' she asked, trying for a friendly tone.

'How long will that take to come?'

'It's rather hard to give a date. The publishers don't like sending just one thing at a time. I have to wait to order until I've twelve titles or so from the same publisher.'

'I'd have thought you would have had a thing like that in stock. Handel's *Messiah* is sung every Christmas, you know, both in Norwich and at the Albert Hall, in London.'

'It's rather hard to keep everybody's interests in mind when you only have room for a small stock.'

'It's not as though you had to depend on the day's catch, though,' said Deben. 'There's nothing here to deteriorate.' He was still unable to find a purchaser for his shop.

In the evenings she put up the shutters, got the orders away, cleared the correspondence on her old typewriter and read The *Bookseller* and *Smith's Trade News*. Completely tired out by the time she went to bed, she no longer dreamed of

46

the heron and the eel, or, so far as she knew, of anything else.

Perhaps her battle to establish herself in the Old House was over, or perhaps she had been wrong in thinking that one had taken place, or would ever take place. But if she was not sure which of these alternatives she meant, the battle could hardly have been decisive.

When the bookshop had been open for three weeks, General Gamart came in unobtrusively. With a sudden pang, she feared he was going to ask for the poems of Charles Sorley; but he, too, wanted the reminiscences of the former SAS man.

'I've often felt like writing down something myself, now that I've got a certain amount of spare time. From the point of view of the infantry, you know – the chap who just walks forward and gets shot.'

She wrapped his purchase carefully. She would have liked to have been instrumental in passing some law which would entail that he would never be unhappy again. But perhaps he ought not really to have been in the shop at all. He was there, at the very least, on sufferance. He glanced about him as though on parole, and retreated with his parcel.

Jessie Welford's sharp niece was somewhat surprised when she drove over for the first time to lend a hand with the books. The turnover was higher than she'd anticipated. There must have been quite a lot of interest in the new venture.

'Shall we just have a look at the transactions?' she asked, clicking her silver Eversharp, and using the tone which brought her employers to heel. 'Three accounts have been opened – the Primary School and the two medical men. Where is your provision for bad debts?'

'I don't know that I've made any,' said Mrs Green.

'It ought to be 5% of what is due to you on the ledger. Then, the depreciation – that should be shown as a debit *here*, and as a credit in the property account. Every debit must have its credit. It is essential that you should be able to see at a glance, at any given time, exactly what you owe and what is owing to you. That is the object of properly kept books. You do want to know that, don't you?'

She guiltily wished she did. If often seemed to her that if she knew exactly what her financial position was down to the last three farthings, as Ivy Welford impressed upon her that she should, she would not have the courage to carry on for another day. She hardly liked to mention that she was thinking of opening a lending library.

The weather had broadened into early summer. 'There's a delivery for you!' Wally sang out from his bike, one foot resting on the pavement. 'He asked the way twice, once at the gasworks, and once at the vicarage. Now he's in trouble turning. He's trying to reverse round in one go, do he'll go straight through your backhouse.'

In time to come this particular van, elegant in its red and cream paint, was to become one of the most familiar in Hardborough. It was from Brompton's, the London store which offered a library service to provincial booksellers, no matter how remote. Summoned by Florence, it brought her first volumes and required her to sign an undertaking and to read the conditions laid down by Brompton's.

These were suggestive of a moral philosophy, or the laws of an ideal state, rather than a business transaction. The books available on loan were divided into classes A, B, and C. A were much in demand, B acceptable, and C frankly old and unwanted. For every A she borrowed, she must take three Bs and a large number of Cs for her subscribers. If she paid more, she could get more As, but also, a mounting pile of Bs and the repellent Cs, and nothing new would be sent until the last consignment was returned.

Bromptons did not offer any suggestions as to how the

subscribers were to be induced to take out the right book. Perhaps, in Knightsbridge, they had their own methods.

When the opening of the lending library was announced, simply by a hand-written notice in the window, thirty of the inhabitants of Hardborough signed up on the first day. Mr Brundish could be considered a certainty. But while he had given no indication at all of what he would like to read, the other thirty were perfectly sure. Comfortably retired or prosperously in business, fond of looking at images of royalty, praisers of things past, they all wanted to have the recent *Life of Queen Mary*. This was in spite of the fact that most of them seemed to possess inner knowledge of the court – more, indeed, than the biographer. Mrs Drury said that the Queen Mother had not done all those embroideries herself, the difficult bits had been filled in for her by her ladies-in-waiting. Mr Keble said that we should not look upon her like again.

Queen Mary was, of course, an A book. In point of time, Mrs Thornton had been the first to put it on her list; and Florence, confident in the justice of her method, placed the Thornton ticket in it. Every subscriber had a pink ticket, and the books were ranged alphabetically, waiting for collection. This was a grave weakness of the system. Everybody knew at a glance what everybody else had got. They should not have been poking about and turning things over in the painfully small space which had been cleared for the library, but they were unused to discipline.

'I think there has been some mistake. I thought I made my choice quite clear. This appears to be a detective story, and not by any means a recent one.' Mrs Keble added that she would be back in half-an-hour. She always thought that things would take about half-an-hour. 'I am not interested in *The History of Chinese Thought* either,' she said.

The library was to open from two to three on Mondays. This was normally the slack time. Mrs Keble really had no business to come so early, but on the point of two o'clock several subscribers came in at once, and the atmosphere, in the cramped back of the shop, at once began to resemble the great historic runs on the Bank of England. During the '45, Mrs Green remembered, the Bank had been forced to hold the customers at bay, to melt down the ink-wells to make bullets and to pay out in sixpences. If only Mrs Thornton would come to take her *Queen Mary* away – but satisfied, perhaps, by her incontestable acquisition of right, she failed, though expected every time the street door opened, to appear. Everyone could see her ticket, 'which, I suppose, means that she is to be allowed to have *Queen Mary* first. I happen to have been told that she is a particularly slow reader, but that isn't really my point.'

'Mrs Thornton asked for the book first. That's the only thing I take into account.'

'Allow me to say, Mrs Green, that if you had a little more experience of committee work you would realize how rash it is to come to a decision as the result of one consideration only. A pity.'

'In a small town we cannot help knowing something of each other. Some of us may be more attached than others to the concept of royalty. Some may feel that they have the *right* to read first about the late Queen Mother. It may have been a loyal devotion of long standing.'

'Mrs Thornton was quite definite about it.' The air of the summer afternoon grew uncomfortably warm. Two more subscribers crowded in, and one of them told Florence, in confidence, that Mrs Thornton was known to have voted Liberal in the last election. Both the backhouse and the street door were now cut off by ladies. At four o'clock – for office hours were short in Hardborough – their husbands joined them.

'I shouldn't have thought it was possible to misunderstand my list. Look, it's written perfectly clearly. It looks like a

50

failure in simple office routine. If everyone wanted this *Life of Queen Mary*, why were not more copies ordered?'

The Old House Bookshop lending library temporarily closed, to reopen in a month, by which time the proprietor hoped to have more assistance. This was an admission of weakness. Wally took a formal note round to Mr Brundish to explain the situation. He hadn't been able to see the old gentleman anywhere; so he gave the note to the milkman, who had left it with the milk under the sacking on the potato clamp, which was where Mr Brundish, whose letter-box had long been rusted up, received his correspondence.

5

I need help – Florence thought – it was folly to think that I could manage all this by myself. She put through a call to the offices of the *Flintmarket, Kingsgrave and Hardborough Times*.

'Can you get it as quickly as possible, Janet?' she asked. She had seen Janet's one-stroke motor-bicycle outside the telephone exchange, and knew she would be in safe hands.

'Are you trying the small ads, Mrs Green?'

'Yes. It's the same number.'

'That won't be worth the money, if you want to advertise for an assistant. One of the Gippings is going to come round to yours after school.'

'A possibility, Janet, but not a certainty.'

'Raven spoke to them about a week ago. He'd have liked to get you the eldest, but she'd have to stay home when Mrs Gipping went to the pea-picking. Or then there's the second one, or the third one.'

She reminded Janet that there might be other subscribers waiting for calls to be put through, but was told that there weren't any.

'The private lines have mostly gone over to Aldeburgh for that music, and the others are at the new fish-and-chip parlour. That opens for the first time tonight.'

'Well, Janet, it might very well catch fire. I believe they use cooking oil. We ought to clear the line for emergencies. Is Mr Deben running it?'

'Oh, no, Deben reckons it'll be the death-blow to his trade. He's attempting to get the Vicar on to his side, saying the odour of frying might waft into the church at Evensong. But the Vicar doesn't like to be drawn into these arguments, he told Deben.'

She wondered what the telephone operators said when they discussed her bookshop.

At teatime next day a little girl of ten years old, very pale, very thin and remarkably fair, presented herself at the Old House. She wore a pair of jeans and a pink cardigan worked in a fancy stitch. Florence recognized her as the child she had seen on the Common.

'You're Christine Gipping, aren't you? I had rather thought that your elder sister . . .'

Christine replied that now the evenings were getting longer her elder sister would be up in the bracken with Charlie Cutts. In fact, she'd just seen their bikes stashed under the bracken by the crossroads.

'You won't have to worry about anything like that with me,' she added. 'I shan't turn eleven till next April. Mine haven't come on yet.'

'What about your other sister?'

'She likes to stay at home and mind Margaret and Peter – that's the little ones. That was a waste giving them those names, it never came to anything between him and the Princess.'

'Please don't get the idea that I don't want to consider you for the job. It's just that you don't really look old enough or strong enough.'

'You can't tell from looking. You look old, but you don't look strong. It won't make much difference, as long as you get someone from ours. We're all of us handy.'

Her skin was almost transparent. Her silky hair seemed to have no substance, ruffling away from her forehead in the slightest draught. When Florence, still anxious not to hurt her feelings, smiled encouragingly, she smiled back, showing two broken front teeth.

They had been broken during the previous winter in rather a strange manner, when the washing on the line froze hard, and she was caught a blow in the face with an icy vest. Like all the Hardborough children, she had learned to endure. Running like tightrope walkers across the narrow handrails of the marsh bridges, they fell and were fractured or half drowned. They pelted each other with stones or with beets from the furrows. A half-witted boy was told that the maggots used as bait would be good for him and make him less dull, and he had eaten a whole jar full. Christine herself looked perilously thin, although Mrs Gipping was known as a good provider.

'I'll come and see your mother tomorrow, Christine, and talk things over.'

'If you want. She'll say I'm to come down every day after school, and Saturdays all day, and you're not to give me less than twelve and six a week.'

'And what about your homework?'

'I'll fare to do that after tea, when I'm at home.'

Christine showed signs of impatience, evidently having decided to start work at once. She deposited her pink cardigan in the backhouse.

'Did you knit that yourself? It looks very difficult.'

'That was in *Woman's Own*,' Christine said, 'but the instructions were for short sleeves.' She frowned, unwilling to admit that she had put on her best to make an impression at the first interview. 'You haven't any children, Mrs Green?'

'No. I should have liked to.'

'Life passed you by in that respect, then.'

Without waiting for explanations she bustled round the shop, opening drawers and finding fault with the arrangements, her faint hair flying. Not enough cards were on display, she declared – she'd see about sorting out some more. And indeed there were large packets of samples still in their wrappers, because Mrs Green hated them, at the back of the drawers.

At first the child's methods were eccentric. With a talent for organization which had long been suppressed by her position as third daughter in the family, she tried the cards first one way, then another. Ignoring the messages, she sorted them largely by colour, so that roses and sunsets were put with a card representing a bright red lobster wearing a Scottish bonnet and raising a glass to its lips with the words '*Just a wee doch an doris afore we gang awa!*' This, certainly, must have been a sample.

'They really ought to be divided into Romantic and Humorous,' said Florence. These, indeed, were the only two attitudes to the stages of life's journey envisaged by the manufacturers of the cards. The lobster took a humorous view of parting. The sunset card was overprinted with a sad message.

'What do "o'er" and "neath" mean?' asked Christine sharply. This first admission that there was something she didn't know encouraged her employer a little. Christine saw immediately that she had lost ground. 'There's a whole lot more you've never even unpacked,' she said reprovingly. They looked together at a brand-new set, naked men and women interlaced, with the caption *Another thing we didn't forget to do today*. 'We'll throw these away,' said Florence firmly. 'Some of the reps have little or no idea of what's suitable.' Christine was doubled up with laughter and said that there were quite a few in Hardborough who wouldn't mind having them through the letter-box. She was well prepared, Florence thought. She would be invaluable when the lending library reopened.

There hardly seemed anything to discuss that evening with Mrs Gipping, who stood tolerantly at her half-open gate when Florence accompanied Christine home.

Little Peter was planting rows of clothes pegs between the rows of early French beans. 'Why's Christine late?' he asked.

'She's been working for this lady.'

'What for?'

'She's got a shop full of books for people to read.'

'What for?'

Now vans and estate cars began to appear in increased numbers over the brilliant horizon of the marshes, sometimes getting bogged down at the crossings and always if they tried to turn round on the foreshore, bringing the publishers' salesmen. Even in summer, it was a hard journey. Those who made it were somewhat unwilling to part with their Fragrant Moments and engagement books, which were what Florence really wanted, unless she would also take a pile of novels which had the air, in their slightly worn jackets, of women on whom no one had ever made any demand. Her fellow-feeling, both for the salesmen and for the ageing books, made her an injudicious buyer. They had come so far, too, that they ought to have tea made for them in the backhouse. There, in the hope that it would be long before they returned to this godforsaken hole, they stirred their sugar and relaxed a little. 'One thing, the competition's not keen. There isn't another point of sale between here and Flintmarket.'

Their hearts sank when they realized that there was no rail-service at all and that all future orders would have to come down by road. By the time they felt that they had to be moving on, the wind had got up, and their vans, without the load which had kept them stable, went weaving to and fro, unable to hold the road. The young bullocks, most inquisitive of all animals, came stepping across the tussocks of grass to stare mildly at them.

'I don't know why I bought these,' Florence reflected after one of these visits. 'Why did I take them? No one used force. No one advised me.' She was looking at 200 Chinese book-markers, handpainted on silk. The stork for longevity, the plum-blossom for happiness. Her weakness for beauty had betrayed her. It was inconceivable that anyone else in Hardborough should want them. But Christine was consoling: the visitors would buy them – come the summer, they didn't know what to spend their money on.

In July, the postman brought a letter postmarked from Bury St Edmund's, but too long, as could easily be seen from the thickness of the envelope, to be an order.

> Dear Madam,
> It may be of interest, and perhaps of entertainment to you, to know how it was that I came to hear of your establishment. A cousin of my late wife's (I should, perhaps, call him a cousin once removed) is connected, through a second marriage, with that coming young man, the Member of Parliament for the Longwash Division, who mentioned to me that at a gathering of his aunt's (Mrs Violet Gamart, who is personally unknown to me) it had been remarked in passing that Hardborough was at last to have a bookshop.

She wondered in what possible way this could be considered entertaining. But she must not be uncharitable.

> It may increase your amusement to learn that I am not writing to you on the subject of books at all!

There were several pages of thin writing paper, from which it emerged that the writer was called Theodore Gill, that he lived somewhere near Yarmouth, and that he was a painter in watercolours who saw no reason to abandon the pleasant style of the turn of the century, and that he would like to organize, or better, have organized for him, a little exhibition of his work at the Old House. The name of Mrs

57

Gamart and of her brilliant nephew would, he was sure, be sufficient recommendation.

Florence looked round at her shelving, behind which scarcely a square foot of wall space could be seen. There was always the oyster warehouse, but even now, in the height of summer, it was damp. She put the letter away in a drawer which already contained several others of the same kind. Later middle age, for the upper middle-class in East Suffolk, marked a crisis, after which the majority became water-colourists, and painted landscapes. It would not have mattered so much if they had painted badly, but they all did it quite well. All their pictures looked much the same. Framed, they hung in sitting-rooms, while outside the windows the empty, washed-out, unarranged landscape stretched away to the transparent sky.

The desire to exhibit somewhere more ambitious than the parish hall accompanied this crisis, and Florence related it to the letters which she also received from 'local authors'. The paintings were called 'Sunset Across the Laze', the books were called 'On Foot Across the Marshes' or 'Awheel Across East Anglia', for what else can be done with flatlands but to cross them? She had no idea, none at all, where she would put the local authors if they came, as they suggested, to sign copies of their books for eager purchasers. Perhaps a table underneath the staircase, if some of the stock could be moved. She vividly imagined their disillusionment, wedged behind the table with books and a pen in front of them, while the hours emptied away and no one came. 'Tuesday is always a very quiet day in Hardborough, Mr ——, particularly if it is fine. I didn't suggest Monday, because that would have been quieter still. Wednesdays are quiet too, except for the market, and Thursday is early closing. The customers will come in and ask for your book soon – of course they will, they have heard of you, you are a local author. Of course they will want your signature, they will come across the marshes, afoot and awheel.' The thought of so much suffering and embarrassment was hard to bear, but at least she was in a position to see that it never took place. She consigned Mr Gill's letter to the drawer.

She had been almost too busy to realize that the holiday season had arrived. Now she noticed that bathing towels hung and flapped at every window of the seafront houses. The ferry crossed the Laze several times every day, the fish-and-chip parlour extended its premises with pieces of corrugated iron transferred from the disused airfield. Wally appeared to ask if Christine would like to come camping, and she wondered if he was not hanging round rather often, and in a marked manner. Christine, however, rejected his invitation with a dignity imitated from her elder sisters. 'That Wally's after your washboard for his skiffle group. I've seen him eyeing it in your backhouse.' 'Then he'd better have it,' Florence said. 'I've never known what to do with it. He can have the mangle too, if he likes.'

She ought to go down to the beach. It was Thursday, early closing, and it seemed ungrateful to live so close to the sea and never to look at it for weeks on end. In fact she preferred the winter beach; but, reproving herself, she had a bathe and then stood in the sun at the end of the long swale of multi-coloured pebbles. Children crouched down to decide which of these pebbles they would put into their buckets; grown men selected others to throw into the sea. The newspapers they brought with them to read had been torn away from them by the wind. The mothers had retreated from the cutting air into the beach huts, which were drawn up in a friendly encampment as far as possible from the coldly encroaching North Sea. Farther to the north unacceptable things had been washed up. Bones were mixed with the fringe of jetsam at high tide. The rotting remains of a seal had been stranded there.

The Hardborough locals mingled fearlessly with the visitors. Florence saw the bank manager, unfamiliar in striped bathing-trunks, with his wife and the chief cashier. He called out, and was understood, in snatches, to say that all work and no play made Jack a dull boy, and that it was the first time he had been able to set foot on the beach this year. No reply was needed. Another voice, from inland, shouted that it had held up bright. Raven was running in his new van. Next week he was going to run some of the sea scouts up to London for their annual day out. They were going to check the progress of Baden-Powell House, and after that they had voted unanimously to go to Liverpool Street Station, and watch the trains go out.

Walking further up the beach was more like plunging at every step. The wet sand and shingle sank as though unwilling to bear her slight weight, and then oozed up again, filling her footprints with glittering water. To leave a mark of any kind was exhilarating. Past the dead seal, past the stretch of pebbles where, eighty years ago, a man had found a piece of amber as big as his head – but no one had ever found amber since then – she reached a desolate tract where the holiday-makers did not venture. A rough path led up and back to the common. Human figures, singly and in pairs, were exercising their dogs. She was surprised to find how many of them were known to her by now as occasional customers. They waved from a distance and then, because the land was so flat and approach was slow, had to wave again as they drew nearer, reserving their smiles until the last moment. With the smiles, most of the exercisers, glad to pause for a moment, said much the same thing: When would the lending library be open again? They had been looking forward to it so much. The dogs, stiff with indignation, dragged sideways at their leads. Florence heard herself making many promises. She felt at a disadvantage without her shoes and wished she had put them on again before leaving the beach for the common.

On wet afternoons, when the heavy weather blew up, the Old House was full of straggling disconsolate holiday parties. Christine, who said that they brought sand into the shop, was severe, pressing them to decide what they wanted. 'Browsing is part of the tradition of a bookshop,' Florence told her. 'You must let them stand and turn things over.' Christine asked what Deben would do if everyone turned over his wet fish. There were finger-marks on some of her cards, too.

Ivy Welford called in to have a look at the books somewhat before her visit was due. Her inquisitiveness was a measure of the shop's success and its reputation outside Hardborough.

'Where are the returns outward?'

'There aren't any,' Florence replied. 'The publishers won't take anything back. They don't like sale or return arrangements.'

'But you've got returns inwards. How is that?'

'Sometimes the customers don't like the books when they've bought them. They're shocked, or say they've detected a distinct tinge of socialism.'

'In that case the price should be credited to your personal account and debited under returns.' It was an accusation of weakness. 'Now, the purchases book. 150 Chinese silk book markers at five shillings each – can that be right?'

'There was a different bird or butterfly on each one. Some of them were rice birds. They were beautiful. That was why I bought them.'

'I'm not questioning that. It's not my concern to ask you how the business is run. My worry is that they're posted in the sales book as having been sold at fivepence each. How do you account for that?'

'It was a mistake on Christine's part. She thought they

were made of paper and misread the price. You can't expect a child of ten to appreciate an Oriental art that has been handed down through the centuries.'

'Perhaps not, but you've failed to show the loss of 4s. 7d. on each article. How am I supposed to prepare a Trial Balance?'

'Couldn't we put it down to petty cash?' pleaded Florence.

'The petty cash should be kept for very small sums. I was just going to ask you about that. What is this disbursement of 12s. 11d.?'

'I daresay it's for milk.'

'You're absolutely certain? Do you keep a cat?'

By September the holiday-makers, with the migrant sea birds, showed the restlessness of coming departure. The Primary School had reopened, and Florence was on her own in the shop for most of the day.

Milo came in and said he would like to buy a birthday present for Kattie. He chose a colouring book of Bible Lands, which Florence considered a mere affectation.

'So Violet isn't going to get her own way,' he said. 'Has she been in here yet?'

'We haven't been open very long.'

'Six months. But she will come. She has far too much self-respect not to.'

Florence felt relieved, and yet obscurely insulted.

'I'm hoping to reopen my lending library quite soon,' she said. 'Perhaps Mrs Gamart – '

'Are you making any money?' Milo asked. There were only two or three other people in the shop, and one of those was a sea scout who came every day after school to read another chapter of *I Flew with the Führer*. He marked the place with a piece of string weighted down with a boiled sweet.

'You really need something like this,' Milo said, not at all urgently. Under his arm he had a thinnish book, covered with the leaf-green paper of the Olympia Press. 'This is volume one.'

'Is there a volume two?'

'Yes, but I've lent it to someone, or left it somewhere.'

'You should keep them together as a set,' said Florence firmly. She looked at the title, *Lolita*. 'I only stock good novels, you know. They don't move very fast. Is this good?'

'It'll make your fortune, Florence.'

'But is it good?'

'Yes.'

'Thank you for suggesting it. I feel the need of advice sometimes. You're very kind.'

'You're always making that mistake,' Milo replied.

The truth was that Florence Green had not been brought up to understand natures such as Milo's. Just as she still thought of gravity as a force that pulled things towards it, not simply as a matter of least resistance, so she felt sure that character was a struggle between good and bad intentions. It was too difficult for her to believe that he simply lapsed into whatever he did next only if it seemed to him less trouble than anything else.

She took a note of the title *Lolita*, and the author's name, Nabokov. It sounded foreign – Russian, perhaps, she thought.

6

Christine liked to do the locking up. At the age of ten and a half she knew, for perhaps the last time in her life, exactly how everything should be done. This would be her last year at the Primary. The shadow of her eleven plus, at the end of the next summer, was already felt. Perhaps, indeed, she ought to give up her job and concentrate on her studies, but Florence, for fear of being misunderstood, could not suggest to her assistant that it might be time for her to leave. The two of them, during the past months, had not been without their effect on one another. If Florence was more resilient, Christine had grown more sensitive.

On the first evening of September that could truthfully be called cold they sat, after the shutters were up, in the front room, in the two comfortable chairs, like ladies. Then the child went to put on the kettle in the backhouse, and Florence listened to the drumming of tap water, followed by a metallic note as the red Coronation tin containing biscuits was banged down on the dresser.

'We've got a blue one at ours. It's Westminster Abbey the same, but the procession goes all the way 'round the tin.'

'I'll light the heater,' said Florence, unused to idleness.

'My mam doesn't think those paraffin heaters are safe.'

'There's no danger as long as you're careful to clean them properly and don't allow a draught from two different sides at once,' Florence replied, screwing the cap of the container hard down. She must be allowed to be in the right sometimes.

The heater did not seem to be quite itself that evening. There was no draught, as far as that could ever be said in

Hardborough; and yet the blue flame shot up for a moment, as though reaching for something, and sank back lower than before. It went by the perhaps extravagant brand name of Nevercold. She had only just managed to get it adjusted when Christine came in seriously with the tea-things, arranged on a large black and gold tray.

'I like this old tray,' she said. 'You can put that down for me in your will.'

'I don't know that I want to think about my will yet, Christine. I'm a business woman in middle life.'

'Did that come from Japan?'

The tray represented two old men, fishing peaceably by moonlight.

'No, it's Chinese lacquer. My grandfather brought it back from Nanking. He was a great traveller. I'm not sure that they know how to make lacquer like this in China any more.'

By now the Nevercold was burning rather more steadily. The teapot basked in front of it, the room grew close, and the difference in age between Christine and Florence seemed less, as though they were no more than two stages of the same woman's life. In Hardborough an evening like this, when the sea could only just be heard, counted as silence. They had, therefore, warmth and quiet; and yet gradually Christine, who had been sitting back, as totally at ease as a rag doll, began to stiffen and fidget. Of course, a child of her age could hardly be expected to sit still for long.

After a while she got up and went into the backhouse – to make sure of the back door, she said. Florence had an impulse to stop her going out of the room, which was proved to be ridiculous when she came back almost immediately. A faint whispering, scratching and tapping could now be heard from the upstairs passage, and something appeared to be dragged hither and thither, like a heavy kitten's toy on a string. Florence did not pretend to herself, any more than she had ever done, that nothing was wrong.

'You're quite comfortable, aren't you, Christine?'

The little girl replied that she was. Unaccountably, she used her 'best' voice, the one urged by her class teacher on those who had to play Florence Nightingale, or the Virgin Mary. She was listening painfully, as though her ears were stretched or pricked.

'I've been wondering if I could help you at all with your eleven plus,' said Florence conversationally. 'Something towards it – I mean, we might read something together.'

'There's no reading to do. They give you some pictures, and you have to say which is the odd one out. Or they give you numbers, like 8, 5, 12, 9, 22, 16 and you have to say which number comes next.'

Just as she had failed to understand Milo, so Florence was unable to tell which number came next. She had been born too long ago. In spite of the Nevercold, the temperature seemed to have dropped perceptibly. She turned the heater up to its highest register.

'You're not cold, are you?'

'I'm always pale,' Christine replied loftily. 'There is no need to turn that thing up for me.' She was trembling. 'My little brother is pale as well. He and I are supposed to be quite alike.'

Neither of them was prepared to say that they wished to protect the other. That would have been to admit fear into the room. Fear would have seemed more natural if the place had been dark, but the bright shop lighting shone into every corner. The muffled din upstairs grew into a turmoil.

'That's coming on loud, Mrs Green.'

Christine had given up her Florence Nightingale voice. Mrs Green took her left hand, which was the nearest. A light current semed to be passing through it, transmitting a cold pulse, as though electricity could become ice.

'Are you sure you're all right?'

The hand lay in hers, weightless and motionless. Perhaps

66

it was dangerous to press the child, and yet Florence overwhelmingly felt that she must make her speak and that something must be admitted between them.

'That's going down my arm like a finger walking,' said Christine slowly. 'That stops at the top of my head. I can feel the hairs standing up properly there.'

It was an admission of sorts. Half rigid, half drowsy, she rocked herself to and fro on the chair in a curious position. The noise upstairs stopped for a moment and then broke out again, this time downstairs and apparently just outside the window, which shook violently. It seemed to be on the point of bursting inwards. Their teacups shook and spun in the saucers. There was a wild rattling as though handful after handful of gravel or shingle was being thrown by an idiot against the glass.

'That's the rapper. My mam knows there's a rapper in this old place. She reckoned that wouldn't start with me, because mine haven't come on yet.'

The battering at the window died to a hiss; then gathered itself together and rose to a long animal scream, again and again.

'Don't mind it, Christine,' Florence called out with sudden energy. 'We know what it can't do.'

'That doesn't want us to go,' Christine muttered. 'That wants us to stay and be tormented.'

They were besieged. The siege lasted for just over ten minutes, during which time the cold was so intense that Florence could not feel the girl's hand lying in hers, or even her own fingertips. After ten minutes, Christine fell asleep.

Florence did not expect her assistant to return; but she came back the very next afternoon, with the suggestion that if they had any more trouble they could both of them kneel down and say the Lord's prayer. Her mother had advised that it would be a waste of time consulting the Vicar. The Gippings were chapel and did not attend St Edmund's, but the minister would be of no use either, as though ghosts could be read down or prayed out, rappers could not. Meanwhile, it must surely be time to wash the dusters.

Florence regretted what seemed a slight on the gracious church whose tower protected the marshes, and whose famous south porch, between its angle buttresses, had been laid in flint checkerwork, silver grey and dark grey, by some ancestor of Mr Brundish. She wished that, when she spoke to the Vicar, the subject did not have to be money. She had been glad to give some of her stock to the harvest festival, although wondering a little how *Every Man His Own Mechanic*, and a pile of novels, could be considered as fruits of the earth and sea. It must be a burden – she realized that only too well – for the Canon to have to devote so much time to fund-raising. She wished she could see him for a moment simply to ask him: Was William Blake right when he said that everything possible to be believed in was an image of Truth. Supposing it was something not possible to be believed in? Did he believe in rappers? Meanwhile she went to the early service at St Edmund's, noticing, on the way out, that it was her turn to do the flowers next week. The list stared at her from the porch: Mrs Drury, Mrs Green, Mrs Thornton, Mrs Gamart for two weeks, as having a larger garden.

Mrs Gipping, whose house was between the old railway station and the church, was pegging up. Seeing Christine's employer walking down from early service, she signalled to her to come into the backhouse. Gipping, glimpsed between rows of green leaves, was tending the early celery, which would stand fit until Christmas.

In the damp warmth of the washday kitchen, Mrs Gipping was reassuring. She had been told about the rapper's visitation; but in her opinion there were disadvantages in every job. 'You'd like a drink, I expect, before you open up your business.' Florence was expecting some Nescafé, to which she had grown accustomed, but was directed to a large vegetable marrow hung over the sink. A wooden spigot had been driven into the rotund and glistening sides of the marrow. It was boldly striped in ripe green and yellow. Cups and glasses were ranged beneath it, and at a turn of the spigot a cloudy liquid oozed out drop by drop and fell heavily into the nearest cup. Mrs Gipping explained that it hadn't been up for long and wasn't at all heady, but that she'd seen a strong man come in and take a drink from a four-week marrow and fall straight down on to the stone floor, so that there was blood everywhere.

'Perhaps you'll give me the recipe,' said Florence politely, but Mrs Gipping replied that she never did, or the Women's Institute, against which she appeared to have some grudge, would go and put it in their collection of Old Country Lore.

Opening the shop gave her, every morning, the same feeling of promise and opportunity. The books stood as neatly ranged as Gipping's vegetables, ready for all comers.

Milo came in at lunch-time. 'Well, are you going to order *Lolita*?'

'I haven't decided yet. I've ordered an inspection copy. I'm confused by what the American papers said about it. One of the reviewers said that it was bad news for the trade and bad news for the public, because it was dull, pretentious, florid and repulsive, but on the other hand there was an article by Graham Greene which said that it was a masterpiece.'

'You haven't asked me what I think about it.'

'What would be the use? You have lost the second volume, or left it somewhere. Did you ever finish reading it?'

'I can't remember. Don't you trust your own judgment, my dear?'

Florence considered. 'I trust my moral judgment, yes. But I'm a retailer, and I haven't been trained to understand the arts and I don't know whether a book is a masterpiece or not.'

'What does your moral judgment tell you about me?'

'That's not difficult,' said Florence. 'It tells me that you should marry Kattie, think less about yourself, and work harder.'

'But you're not sure about *Lolita*? Are you afraid that the little Gipping girl might read it?'

'Christine? Not in the least. In any case, she never reads the books. She's an ideal assistant in that way. She only reads *Bunty*.'

'Or that the Gamarts mightn't like it? Violet still hasn't been here, has she?'

Milo added that the General had told him, when their cars were both waiting at the Flintmarket level crossing, that his wife didn't expect *Lolita* would ever be sold in a dear, sleepy little place like Hardborough.

'I don't want to take any of these things into account. If *Lolita* is a good book, I want to sell it in my shop.'

'It would make money, you know, if the worst came to the worst.'

'That isn't the point,' Florence replied, and really it was not. She wondered why this matter of the worst coming to the worst seemed to recur. Only a few days ago, down on the marshes, Raven had shown her a patch of green succulent weeds which, he said, were considered a delicacy in London and would fetch a high price if they were sent up there. 'That might help you, Mrs Green, if things don't work out.'

'We're doing quite respectably at the moment,' she told Milo. 'I shall take good advice about *Lolita* when the time comes.'

Milo seemed vaguely dissatisfied. 'I should like to read *Bunty*,' he said. Florence told him that there was a large pile of *Bunties* in the backhouse, but she couldn't part with any of them without Christine's permission, and school wasn't out until half-past three.

After six months of trading Florence calculated that she had £2,500 worth of stock in hand, was owed about £80 on outstanding accounts and had a current bank balance with Mr Keble of just over £400 – a working capital of £3,000. She lived largely on tea, biscuits, and herrings and had spent almost nothing on advertising, except, for she couldn't disoblige the Vicar, in the parish magazine. Her wages bill was still twelve and sixpence a week, thirty shillings during the holidays. She didn't allow discount, except to the Primary School. Despatch was not at all the same as it had been at Müller's. The inhabitants were all used to dropping things in as they passed by. Everyone on two or four wheels, not only the obliging Wally, was a potential carrier. She herself was going to take the ferry across the Laze, as it was early-closing day, to deliver thirty Complete Wild Flower Recognition Handbooks to the Women's Institute. Remembering this, she took the top book off the crisp pile and looked through the illustrations for the green marsh plant which Raven had shown to her. It was not mentioned.

7

Eventually Mrs Gamart did come to the Old House Book-shop. It was a fortnight after the library re opened, this time at a much calmer tempo, as though the subscribers had restrained themselves and the atmosphere had mellowed with the advancing year.

Christine had grasped the system rapidly and had made short work of learning the names of subscribers she did not know, that is, those who lived outside Hardborough. She classified them by attributes – Mrs Birthmark, Major Wheezer, and so forth – just as Raven did to tell the cattle apart; otherwise he'd never know the strays. Their correct names followed, and in remembering what books they had asked for, and what in fact they were going to get, the child was unerring. Impartiality made her severe. The library did not open now until school was out, and under her régime no one was allowed so much as to look at anyone else's selection.

The late autumn weather made the little expedition to the library just about the right length for the retired, both for those who drove and walked and for those who pottered. They seemed to be prepared to accept the B books, and even the Cs, without much complaint.

Mrs Gamart opened the street door on an afternoon at the end of October. The sun had gone round, and her shadow preceded her down the steps. She wore a three-quarter length Jaeger camel coat. Florence recognized the moment as a crisis in her fortunes. She had been too busy lately to think about the pressure that had been put upon her, six months earlier, to leave the Old House – or rather, to be honest, she kept herself busy so that the thought would not be uppermost in her mind. It was uppermost now. The shop had been transformed into a silent battleground in a nominal state of truce. She was in authority, on her own ground, and with some kind of support, since Christine had arrived and was depositing her Wellingtons and cardigan in the backhouse. On the other hand, Mrs Gamart, as a customer, must be deferred to; and as a patroness she was in the unassailable position of having forgiven all. She had made a request in the name of the Arts, and it had been refused; the Old House was still a shop, and yet she continued to behave with smiling dignity.

The library section was full of mildly loitering subscribers. There were customers in the front of the shop as well.

'I can see you're very busy. Please don't put yourself out. I really came to have a look at your library, just to see how it works. I've been meaning to do it for so long.'

Christine, by arrangement, looked after the issues and library tickets, particularly if several people were waiting. Glad to be indispensable, she was combing out her pale hair, tugging at the knots, and energetically ready to take over. Then, more or less tidy, she sprang out of the backhouse with the enthusiasm of a terrier empowered, for the afternoon, to act as a sheepdog. With rapid fingers she began to flick through the pink tickets. 'Just a tick, Mrs Keble. I'll fare to look after all of you in turn.' This would not quite do for Mrs Gamart's first visit, and Florence left the cash desk to escort her and to explain the system personally. At that moment she felt herself grasped forcibly by the elbow. Something with a sharp edge caught her in the small of the back.

It was the corner of a picture frame. She was held back by an urgent hand, and addressed by a man, not young, in a corduroy jacket, smiling as a toad does, because it has no other expression. The smile was, perhaps, 'not quite right'.

73

He had been manhandling a large canvas down the steps. Other smaller canvases were under his arm.

'You remember my letter. Theodore Gill, painter in watercolours, very much at your service. The possibility of an exhibition . . . a small selection of my work – poor things, madam, but mine own.'

'I didn't answer your letter.'

There were frames and sketches everywhere. How could they have invaded the shop so quickly?

'But silence means consent. Not as much room as I anticipated, but I can arrange for the loan of some screens from a very good friend, himself a watercolourist of note.'

'He doesn't want to exhibit too, I hope?'

'Later – you are very quick to understand me – but later.'

'Mr Gill, this isn't the best time to discuss your pictures. My shop is open to everyone, but I'm busy at the moment, and now that you've seen the Old House you'll realize that I've no room at all for your exhibition or anyone else's.'

'Sunset Viewed from Hardborough Common Across the Laze,' Mr Gill interrupted, raising his voice. 'Of local interest! Westward, look, the land is bright!'

All this time, beyond the scope of her immediate attention, a murmur of unease, even something like a shout, was rising from the back of the room. As she attempted, in an undignified scuffle, to prevent Mr Gill from tacking up his sunset, she became aware, for the first time, of a breaking up and surging forward of ranks. Mrs Gamart, very red in the face, one hand oddly clasped in the other, and possessed by some strong emotion, passed rapidly throught the shop and left without a word.

'What is it? What happened?'

Christine followed, redder still. Indeed her cheeks were red as fire and beginning to be streaked with tears.

'Mrs Gamart from The Stead, she wouldn't wait her turn, she picked up other people's books and looked at them. Do they were hers she wasn't allowed to do that, and she's muddled my pink tickets!'

'What did you do, Christine?'

'You wanted me to do it orderly! I gave her a good rap over the knuckles.'

She was still holding her school ruler, ornamented with a series of Donald Ducks. In the flow and counterflow of indignation, Mr Gill succeeded in hanging several more of his little sketches. The subscribers clamoured against the poor judgment shown. They had always known it was folly to entrust so much to a child of ten. Look, she was in tears. Mrs Gamart had suffered actual physical violence, and one of the customers tried to make off with a card and envelope. He said he had despaired of getting proper attention. Florence charged him 6¾d. and rang it up on the till; and that was her sole proft for the afternoon.

If she had gone out immediately into the High Street and apologized, the situation might have been retrieved. But she judged that the most important thing was to console Christine. Of course the subscribers had been right, the girl had been given too much authority, a poison, like any other excess. The only remedy, however, in this case was to give her more.

'I don't want you to think any more about it.' But, Christine blubbered, they had gone off with their pink tickets, and without their books. She mourned the destruction of a system.

'But there's still this one for Mr Brundish. He'll be waiting. I'm relying on you to take it round to him as usual.'

Christine put on her cardigan and anorak.

'I'll leave it for him where I always do, by the milk bottles. What are you going to do with all those old pictures?'

Mr Gill had gone to seek, as he put it, a cup of tea, which he wouldn't find any nearer than the Ferry Café. That, too, might well be shut in October. He might be grievously disappointed, possibly after a lifetime of disappointments. Florence would have to find time to mind about that, and indeed about a number of things; but all she wanted at the moment was to think of something which would give more dignity to Christine's errand.

'Wait a moment. There's a letter I want you to take as well, a letter to Mr Brundish. It won't take me long to write it.'

That morning the post had brought the inspection copy of *Lolita*. She took off the jacket and looked at the black cover, stamped in silver.

Dear Mr Brundish,

Your letter to me when I first opened this shop was a great encouragement, and I am venturing now to ask for your advice. Your family, after all, has been living in Hardborough a great deal longer than anyone else's. I don't know if you have heard of the novel which Christine Gipping is bringing with this note – *Lolita*, by Vladimir Nabokov. Some critics say that it is pretentious, dull, florid and repulsive; others call it a masterpiece. Would you be good enough to read it and to let me know whether you think I should be doing right in ordering it and recommending it to my customers?

Yours sincerely,

Florence Green.

'Will there be an answer, then?' asked Christine doubtfully.

'Not today. But in a few days, a week or so perhaps, I'm sure there will.'

The lending library did not close the next week, but continued business in a hushed and decorous fashion. Theodore Gill, with his seemingly endless reserves of watercolours, had been evacuated. This was a bold stroke. Rhoda

Dressmaker's, next door, was certainly not an old house, and it was perhaps a pity that it had been refaced with pebble-dash and the window-frames painted mauve, but it had an excellent, well-lighted showroom.

'You've got such nice clear walls, Jessie,' Florence began diplomatically. 'I don't know whether you've ever felt the need of a few pictures?'

'A semi-permanent exhibition,' put in Mr Gill, who was wandering about as usual. He would ruin everything.

'No, just a few watercolours for the time being. Perhaps one or two each side of your Silent Memories Calendar,' said Florence, who had supplied the calendar at cost price.

Jessie Welford did not answer directly, but turned to the artist himself. 'I never really think a wall needs anything, but I'm prepared to oblige if you're in a difficulty.'

He was hammering and banging all afternoon; the noise was almost as irritating as the poltergeist. Jessie's deprecatory laugh could also be heard. A card advertising the exhibition was placed in Rhoda's window. Jessie continued to laugh, and said that she had never had anything to do with an artist before, but that there had to be a first time for everything.

Florence had not considered how the answer to her note might come. She had certainly not expected it to be conveyed by Mrs Gipping. But Christine's mother, standing in front of her next day at the grocer's, told her suddenly and quite frankly that she was buying a pound of mixed fruit because Mr Brundish had told her to leave a cake for him on Sunday. He'd made up his mind, and she might as well pass this on now and save trouble, to ask Florence to tea on that day. In this way what was presumably a device to gain a measure of privacy became known to the whole of Hardborough. It was so improbable as to be almost frightening. Nobody, except an occasional mysterious old friend from Cambridge or London, ever received such an invitation. This, no doubt, was why Mrs Gipping had not wanted to waste her news on a smaller public.

To go there would be to increase the misunderstanding with Mrs Gamart, still unacknowledged at Holt House. Perhaps this was vanity. What could it matter where she went? An instinct, perhaps a shopkeeper's instinct, told her that it would matter. She hesitated. But an oddly-expressed reply from Mr Brundish, conveyed by Wally, and mentioning honour, convenience, and a-quarter-to-five exactly on Sunday afternoon, decided her. He told her that he had given careful consideration to what she had asked him, and hoped she would be satisfied with his answer.

The beginning of November was one of the very few times of the year when there was no wind. On the evening of the 5th a large bonfire was lit on the hard, near the moorings on the estuary. The pile of fuel had stood there for days, like a giant heron's nest. It was a joint undertaking about which every parent in Hardborough was prepared to give advice. Diesel fuel, although it was said to have burnt someone's eyebrows off last year, and they had never grown again, was used to start it. Then the sticks caught. Gathered up and down the shore, coated with sea-salt, they exploded into a bright blue flame. The otters and water-rats fled away up the dykes; the children came nearer, gathering from every quarter of the common. Potatoes were baked for them in the fire, coming out thick with ashes. The potatoes also tasted of diesel fuel. The organizers of the bonfire, once it had got going, stood back from the cavernous glow and discussed the affairs of the day. Even the headmaster of the Technical, who kept an eye on the blaze in a semi-official capacity, even Mrs Traill from the Primary, even the dejected-looking Mrs Deben, knew where Florence was going to tea on the Sunday.

* * *

She was not even sure how to get into Holt House. There was an iron bell-pull on the right of the front door, she told herself, as she set out. She had noticed it often. It was ornamental and massive and looked as though it might pull away leaving a length of chain in the visitor's hand. What a fool one would look then.

But the front door, when she got there, was not locked. It opened on to a hall lit dimly from a cupola, two floors above. The light struck the sluggish glass of a large Venetian mirror on the dark red wallpaper, patterned with darker red. Just inside the door stood a bronze statue of a fox-terrier, rather larger than life size, sitting up and begging, with a lead in its mouth. The lead was of real leather. On the hall chest there were porcelain jars, balls of string, and a bowl of yellowing visiting cards. The strong scent of camphor came perhaps from this chest, which stood against the left-hand wall. 'It formerly contained a croquet set,' said a voice in the gloom, 'but there is not much opportunity to play nowadays.'

Mr Brundish came forwards, looking critically round the hall, as though it were an outlying province of his territory which he rarely visited. His head turned gradually and suspiciously from side to side on his short neck. A clean white shirt was all that could properly be made out in the gloom. The collar seemed like the entrance to a burrow into which his dark face retreated, while his dark eyes watched anxiously.

'Come into the dining-room.'

The dining-room was straight through, with French windows closed on the garden. The view outside was blocked by a beech hedge, still hanging with brown leaves, heavy in the November damp. A mahogany table stretched from end to end of the room. Florence felt sad to think of anyone eating alone at such a table. It was laid, evidently for the occasion, with an assortment of huge blue-and-white earthenware dishes, looking like prizes at a fairground. Lost among them was a fruit-cake, a bottle of milk and an unpleasantly pink ham, still in its tin.

'We should have a cloth,' said Mr Brundish, taking the starched white linen out of a drawer, and trying to sweep the giant crockery aside. This Florence prevented by sitting down herself. Her host immediately took his place, huddling into a wing chair, spreading his large neat hairy hands on each side of his plate. Shabby, hardly presentable, he was not the sort of figure who could ever lose dignity. He was waiting, with a certain humility, for her to pour out. The silver teapot was the size of a small font, awkward to lift, and almost stone cold. Round the crest ran a motto: *Not to succeed in one thing is to fail in all*.

Fortunately, since there was only one knife on the table and the forks had been forgotten, Mr Brundish made no attempt to press the cake or the ham on his guest. Nor did he drink his cooling tea. Florence wondered whether, as a general rule, he had any regular meals at all. He wanted to welcome her but was more used to threatening, and the change of attitude was difficult for him. She felt the appeal of this. After a period of absolute silence which was not embarrassing because he was evidently so used to it, Mr Brundish said:

'You asked me a question.'

'Yes, I did. It was about a new novel.'

'You paid me the compliment of asking me a serious question,' Mr Brundish repeated heavily. 'You believed that I would be impartial. Doubtless you thought that I was quite alone in the world. That, as it happens, is not so. Otherwise I should be an interesting test case to establish whether there is such a thing as an action which harms no one but oneself. Such problems interested me in younger days. But, as I say, I am not alone. I am a widower, but I had brothers, and one sister. I still have relations and direct descendants, although they are scattered over the face of the globe. Of course, one can have enough of that sort of thing. Perhaps it strikes you that this tea is not quite hot.'

Florence sipped gallantly. 'You must miss your grand-children.'

Mr Brundish considered this carefully. 'Am I fond of children?' he asked.

She realized that the question was simply the result of lack of practice. He talked so seldom to people that he had forgotten the accepted forms of doing so.

'I shouldn't have thought so,' she said, 'but *I* am.'

'One of the Gipping girls, the third one, helps you in your shop, I believe. And that is all the assistance you get.'

'I have a book-keeper who comes in from time to time, and then there is my solicitor.'

'Tom Thornton. You won't get much out of him. In twenty-five years of practice I've never heard of his taking a case to counsel, or even to court. He always settles. Never settle!'

'There's no question of any legal proceedings. That wasn't at all what I wanted to ask you about.'

'I daresay Thornton would refuse to come to your place in any case. It's haunted, and he wouldn't care for that. Perhaps, by the way, you would have liked a wash. There is a lavatory on the right side of the hall with several basins. In my father's day it was particularly useful for shooting parties.'

Florence leant forward. 'You know, Mr Brundish, there is a certain responsibility about trying to run a bookshop.'

'I believe so, yes. Not everybody approves of it, you know. There are certain people, I think, who don't. I am referring to Violet Gamart. She had other plans for the Old House, and now it seems that she has been affronted in some way.'

'I'm sure she knows that was an accident.' It was difficult to speak anything other than the truth in Holt House, but Florence added, 'I'm sure that she means well.'

'Means well! Think again!' He tapped on the table with a weighty teaspoon. 'She wants an Arts Centre. How can the arts have a centre? But she thinks they have, and she wishes to dislodge you.'

'Even if she did,' said Florence, 'it wouldn't have the slightest effect on me.'

'It appears to me that you may be confusing force and power. Mrs Gamart, because of her connections and acquaintances, is a powerful woman. Does that alarm you?'

'No.'

Mr Brundish ignored, or perhaps had never been taught, the polite convention of not staring. He did stare. He looked fixedly at Florence, as though surprised at her being there at all, and yet she felt encouraged by his single-minded concentration.

'May I go back to my first question? I am thinking of making a first order of two hundred and fifty copies of *Lolita*, a considerable risk; but of course I'm not consulting you in a business sense – that would be quite wrong. All I should like to know, before I put in the order, is whether you think it is a good book, and whether it is right for me to sell it in Hardborough.'

'I don't attach as much importance as you do, I dare say, to the notions of right and wrong. I have read *Lolita*, as you requested. It is a good book, and therefore you should try to sell it to the inhabitants of Hardborough. They won't understand it, but that is all to the good. Understanding makes the mind lazy.'

Florence sighed with relief at a decision in which she had had no part. Then, to reassure herself of her independence, she took the single knife, cut two pieces of cake, and offered one to Mr Brundish. Deeply preoccupied, he put the slice on his plate as gently as if he were replacing a lid. He had something to say, something closer to his intentions in asking her to his house than anything that had gone before.

'Well, I have given you my opinion. Why should you think that a man would be a better judge of these things than a woman?'

At these words a different element entered the conversation, as perceptible as a shift in wind. Mr Brundish made no attempt to check this, on the contrary he seemed to be relieved that some prearranged point had been reached.

'I don't know that men are better judges than women,' said Florence, 'but they spend much less time regretting their decisions.'

'I have had plenty of time to make mine. But I have never found it difficult to come to conclusions. Let me tell you what I admire in human beings. I value most the one virtue which they share with gods and animals, and which need not therefore be referred to as a virtue. I refer to courage. You, Mrs Green, possess that quality in abundance.'

She knew perfectly well, sitting in the dull afternoon light, with the ludicrous array of slop basins and tureens in front of her, that loneliness was speaking to loneliness, and that he was appealing to her directly. The words had come out slowly, as though between each one she was being given the opportunity of a response. But while the moment hung in the balance and she struggled to put some kind of order into what she felt or half guessed, Mr Brundish sighed deeply. Perhaps he had found her wanting in some respect. His direct gaze turned gradually away from her, and he looked down at his plate. The necessity to make conversation returned.

'This cake would have been poison to my sister,' he observed.

Not long after, and not daring to make any suggestions about washing up, Florence took her leave. Mr Brundish accompanied her back across the hall. It was quite dark, and she wondered whether he would sit alone in the dark, or

83

whether he would soon turn on the lights. He wished her good fortune, as he had done before, with her enterprise.

'I mustn't let myself worry,' she said. 'While there's life, there's hope.'

'What a terrifying thought that is,' muttered Mr Brundish.

British Railways delivered the copies of *Lolita* from Flintmarket station, twenty-five miles away. When the carrier van arrived it drew, as usual, a ragged cheer from the bystanders. Something new was coming to Hardborough. Outside every public house there were parcels waiting to go out, and Raven, to save petrol, wanted a lift to the upper marshes.

Christine was aghast at the large numbers ordered. They hadn't sold so many of any one thing, not even *Build Your Own Racing Dinghy*. And it was long – four hundred pages. Yet she admired her employer's integrity and seeming excess. Florence told her that the book was already famous. 'Everyone will have heard of it. They may not expect to be able to buy it here in Hardborough.'

'They won't expect to find two hundred and fifty copies. You've lost your head properly over this.'

They closed earlier than usual so that they could re-dress the window. Behind the shutters they arranged the *Lolita*s in pyramids, like the tins in the grocer's. All the old Sellers were put in with the Stayers, and the dignified Illustrateds and flat books were shifted and disturbed without respect. 'What's all this cash in the till?' Christine asked. 'You've got a float of nearly fifty pounds in here.' But Florence had drawn it specially, being pretty sure that she would need it all. The cashier looked up at her with suspended animation, waiting until she had left the bank to see what Mr Keble thought about it.

8

December 4 1959

Dear Mrs Green,

I am in recept of a letter from John Drury & Co, representing their client Mrs Violet Gamart of The Stead, to the effect that your current window display is attracting so much undesirable attention from potential and actual customers that it is providing a temporary obstruction unreasonable in quantum and duration to the use of the highway, and that his client intends to establish a particular injury to herself in that it is necesary that she, as a Justice of the Peace and Chairwoman of numerous committees (list enclosed herewith) has to carry out her shopping expeditiously. In addition, the regular users of your lending library, who, you must remember, are legally in the position of invitees, have found themselves inconvenienced and in some cases been crowded or jostled and in other instances referred to by strangers to the district as old dears, old timers, old hens, and even old boilers. The civil action, which remains independent of course of any future police action to abate the said nuisance, might result in the award of considerable damages against us.

> Yours faithfully,
>
> Thomas Thornton,
>
> Solicitor and Commissioner for Oaths.

December 5 1959

Dear Mr Thornton,

   You have been my solicitor now for a number of years, and I understand 'acting for me' to mean 'acting energetically on my behalf'. Have you been to see the window display for yourself? We are very busy indeed on the sales side at the moment, but if you could manage the 200 yards down the road you might call into the shop and tell me what you think of it.

Yours sincerely,

Florence Green.

December 5 1959

Dear Mrs Green,

   In reply to your letter of 5 December, which rather surprised me by its tone, I have endeavoured on two separate occasions to approach your front window, but found it impossible. Customers appear to be coming from as far away as Flintmarket. I think that we shall have to grant that the obstruction is unreasonable, at least as regards quantum. As to your other remarks, I would advise that it would be as well for you, as well as for myself, to keep a careful record of what has passed between us.

Yours faithfully,

Thomas Thornton,

Solicitor and Commissioner for Oaths.

December 6 1959

Dear Mr Thornton,
   What do you advise, then?

Yours sincerely,

Florence Green.

December 8 1959

Dear Mrs Green,

In reply to your letter of 6 December, I think we ought to abate the obstruction, by which I mean stopping the general public from assembling in the narrowest part of the High Street, before any question of an indictment arises, and I also think we should cease to offer for sale the complained-of and unduly sensational novel by V. Nabokov. We cannot cite Herring v. Metropolitan Board of Works 1863 in this instance as the crowd has not assembled as the result of famine or of a shortage of necessary commodities.

> Yours faithfully,
> Thomas Thornton,
> Solicitor and Commissioner for Oaths.

December 9 1959

Dear Mr Thornton,

A good book is the precious life-blood of a master-spirit, embalmed and treasured up on purpose to a life beyond life, and as such it must surely be a necessary commodity.

> Yours sincerely,
> Florence Green.

December 10 1959

To: Mrs Florence Green

Dear Madam,

I can only repeat my former advice, and I may add that in my opinion, although this is a personal matter

and therefore outside my terms of reference, you
would do well to make a formal apology to Mrs
Gamart.

Yours faithfully,

Thomas Thornton,

Solicitor and Commissioner for Oaths.

December 11 1959

Dear Mr Thornton,
  Coward!

Yours sincerely,

Florence Green.

If Florence was courageous, it was in quite a different way
from, for example, General Gamart, who had behaved
exactly the same when he was under fire as when he wasn't,
or from Mr Brundish, who defied the world by refusing to
admit it to his earth. Her courage, after all, was only a
determination to survive. The police, however, did not
prosecute, or even consider doing so, and after Drury had
advised Mrs Gamart that there was nothing like enough
evidence to proceed on, the complaint was dropped. The
crowd grew manageable, the shop made £82 10s. 6d. profit
in the first week of December on *Lolita* alone, and the new
customers came back to buy the Christmas orders and the
calendars. For the first time in her life, Florence had the
alarming sensation of prosperity.

She might have felt less secure if she had reviewed the
state of her alliances. Jessie Welford and the watercolour
artist, who by now was a permanent lodger at Rhoda's, were
hostile. Christine's comment, that she'd as soon go to bed
with a toad as with that Mr Gill, and she was surprised he
didn't give Miss Welford warts, was quite irrelevant; the fact

was that the two made front together. Not one of the throng in the High Street had come into the dressmaker's, still less bought a watercolour. Nor had they looked at the wet fish offered by Mr Deben. All the tradespeople were now either slightly or emphatically hostile to the Old House Bookshop. It was decided not to ask her to join the Inner Wheel of the Hardborough and District Rotary Club.

As Christmas approached, she grew reckless. She took her affairs out of Mr Thornton's wavering hands and entrusted them to a firm of solicitors in Flintmarket. Through the new firm she contracted with Wilkins, who undertook building as well as plumbing, to pull down the damp oyster warehouse – work, it must be admitted, which went ahead rather slowly. She could decide later what to do with the site. Then, to make room for the new stock, she turned out, on an impulse, the mouldering piles of display material left by the publishers' salesmen. A life-size cardboard Stalin and Roosevelt and an even larger Winston Churchill, an advancing Nazi tank to be assembled in three pieces and glued lightly on the dotted line, Stan Matthews and his football to be suspended from the ceiling with the string provided, six-foot cards of footsteps stained with blood, a horse with moving eyeballs jumping a fence, easily worked with a torch battery, menacing photographs of Somerset Maugham and Wilfred Pickles. All out, all to be given to Christine, who wanted them for the Christmas Fancy Dress Parade.

This was an event organized by local charities. 'I'm obliged to you for these, Mrs Green,' Christine said. 'Otherwise I'd have fared to go attired as an Omo packet.' The detergent firms were prepared to send quantities of free material, as were the *Daily Herald* and the *Daily Mirror*. But everyone in Hardborough was sick of these disguises. Florence wondered why the young girl didn't want to go dressed as something pretty, perhaps as a Pierrette. Out of the unpromising materials, however, Christine sewed and glued together an odd but striking costume – Good-bye, 1959. One of the *Lolita* jackets provided a last touch, and Florence, whose feet were almost as small as her assistant's, lent a pair of shoes. They were crocodile courts, the buckles also covered with crocodile. Christine, who had never seen them before, although she had had a good poke round upstairs, wondered if they were by Christian Dior.

'You know that Dior met a gipsy who told him he'd have ten years of good fortune and then meet his death,' she said. Florence felt she could hardly afford to speak lightly of the supernatural.

'That'd be a French gipsy, of course,' said Christine consolingly, slopping about in the crocodile courts.

The patroness of the Fancy Dress Parade was Mrs Gamart, from The Stead. The judge, in deference to his connection with the BBC, and therefore with the Arts, was Milo North, who protested amiably that he should never have been asked, as he tried to avoid definite judgments on every occasion. His remarks were greeted with roars of laughter. The Parade was held in the Coronation Hall, never quite completed as Hardborough had intended, so that the roof was still of corrugated iron. The rain pounded down, only quietening as it turned to drizzle or sleet. Christine Gipping, wheeling Melody in a pram decorated with barbed wire, which had been sent down to publicize *Escape or Die*, was an easy winner of the most original costume. Discussion on the point was hardly possible.

The Nativity Play, which followed a week later, was on a Saturday afternoon, when the shop was too busy with the Christmas trade for Florence to take time off. She heard about the performance, however, from Wally and Raven, who dropped in, and Mrs Traill, who had come to see about her orders for next term.

The critical reception of the play had been mixed. Too much realism, perhaps, had been attempted when Raven

90

had brought a small flock of sheep off the marshes on to the stage. On the other hand, no one had forgotten their parts, and Christine's dancing had been the success of the evening. As a result of her success in the Fancy Dress she had been awarded the coveted part of Salome, which meant that she was entitled to appear in her eldest sister's bikini.

'She had to dance, to get the head of John the Baptist,' Wally explained.

'What music did you have?' asked Florence.

'That was a Lonnie Donegan recording, Putting on the Agony, Putting on the Style. I don't know that you cared for it very much, Mrs Traill.'

Mrs Traill replied that after many years at the Primary she had become accustomed to everything. 'Mrs Gamart, I'm afraid, didn't look as though she approved.'

'If she didn't, there was nothing she could do about it,' Raven said. 'She was powerless.' He exuded a warm glow of well-being, having had one or two at the Anchor on the way over.

Florence was still anxious about Christine's prospects in the eleven plus. 'She is such a good little assistant, I can't help feeling that after she's been through grammar school she might make it her career. She has the ability to classify, and that can't be taught.'

The glance that flashed through Mrs Traill's spectacles suggested that everything could be taught. Nevertheless, a sense of responsibility weighed on Florence. She felt she ought to have done more. Granted that the child didn't like reading, with the exception of *Bunty*, or being read to, mightn't there be other opportunities? She kept Wally back after the others had gone and said that she had been interested to hear about the play, but had he or his friends or Christine ever been to a real theatre? They might go over to the Maddermarket, at Norwich, if something good came on.

'We've none of us ever been there,' Wally replied doubt-fully, 'but we did go over from the school to Flintmarket last year, to see a travelling company. That was quite interesting, to see how they fixed up the amplification.'

'What play did they put on?' asked Florence.

'The day we went it was *Hansel and Gretel*. There's singing in it. They didn't do it all – they did the bit where the boy and girl lie down and get fresh together, and the angels come in and cover them with leaves.'

'You didn't understand the play, Wally. Hansel and Gretel are brother and sister.'

'That doesn't make it any different, Mrs Green.'

January, as always, brought its one day when people said that it felt like spring. The sky was a patched and ragged blue, and the marsh, with its thousand weeds and grasses, breathed a faint odour of resurrection.

Florence went for her walk in a direction she usually avoided, perhaps not deliberately, but certainly she had not been that way for a long time. Turning her back on the estuary of the Laze, she walked over the headland, north-wards. A notice on a wired-up gate read PRIVATE: FARM LAND. She knew that the path was a right of way, climbed over, and went on. Presently it took a sharp turn to the sea, which idled on its stony beach, forty feet below. The turf was as springy as fine green hair. Running to the cliff's edge could be seen the ghost of an old service road, and on each side of it were ruins, ruins of bungalows and more ambitious small villas. A whole estate had been built there five years ago without any calculation of the sea's erosion. Before anyone had come to live there the sandy cliff had given way and the houses had begun to totter and slide. Some of the FOR SALE FREEHOLD notices were still in place. One of the smaller villas was left right on the verge. Half the foundations and the front wall were gone, while the sitting-room, exposed to all the birds of the air, flapped its last shreds of wallpaper over the void.

For ten minutes or so – since it felt like spring – Florence sat on an abandoned front doorstep, laid with ornamental tiles. The North Sea emitted a brutal salt smell, at once clean and rotten. The tide was running out fast, pausing at the submerged rocks and spreading into yellowish foam, as though deliberating what to throw up next or leave behind, how many wrecks of ships and men, how many plastic bottles. It annoyed her that she could not remember exactly, although she had been told often enough, how much of the coast was eroded every year. Wally would supply the information immediately. Churches with peals of bells were under those waves, as well as the outskirts of a speculative building estate. Historians dismissed the legend, pointing out that there would have been plenty of time to save the bells, but perhaps they didn't know Hardborough. How many years had they left the Old House, when everyone knew it was falling to pieces?

Milo and Kattie – someone young, in any case, with bright red tights, so it could hardly be anyone else – were walking down the cliff path. When they got nearer, Florence could see that Kattie looked as though she had been crying, so the outing could hardly have been a success.

'Why are you sitting on a doorstep, Florence?' Milo asked.

'I don't know why I go out for walks at all. Walks are for the retired, and I'm going to go on working.'

'Is there room on your step for me to sit down?' Kattie asked. She was behaving nicely, trying to please and conciliate. Either she wanted Milo to see how readily she could charm other people, or she wanted to show him how kind she could be to a dull middle-aged woman, simply because Milo seemed to know her. Whichever it was, Florence felt deeply sympathetic. She made room on the step at once and

93

Kattie sat down neatly, pulling her short skirt down over her long red legs.

'Kattie wouldn't believe that there were ruins in Hardborough, so I brought her to see,' said Milo, looking down at both of them, and then at the pitiful houses. 'They were all ready to move into, weren't they? I wonder if the water's still connected.' He stepped over a pile of masonry into the remains of a kitchenette, and tried the taps. Rusty water, the colour of blood, gushed out. 'Kattie could live here perfectly well. She keeps saying she doesn't like our place.'

Florence, wishing to change the subject, asked Kattie about her work at the BBC. It was rather disappointing to find that she had nothing to do with television but checked the expenses sheets for the Recorded Programmes Department, which she referred to as RPD. Surely that couldn't be rewarding work for this intelligent-looking girl.

'We've been to lunch with Violet Gamart,' said Milo, balancing easily on the short grass at the very edge of the cliff. 'It was a chance for her not to disapprove of us.'

'Why can't you ever say anything agreeable about anybody?' Florence asked. 'Does she still want you to run, or look as though you're running, an Arts Centre in Hardborough?'

'That's a seasonal matter with her. It reaches a serious crisis every summer, when Glyndebourne and the Aldeburgh Festival get into the news. Now it's January. The pulse is low.'

'Mrs Gamart was very kind,' said Kattie, hugging herself rather as Christine sometimes did.

'I don't like kind people, except for Florence.'

'That doesn't impress me,' said Florence. 'You appear to me to work less and less. You must remember that the BBC is a Corporation, and that your salary is ultimately met out of public funds.'

'That's Kattie's business,' Milo replied. 'She does my expense sheets. We'll walk back with you.'

'Thank you, I'll stay here for a little longer.'

'Please come with us,' said Kattie. She appeared to be racking her brains. 'Won't you tell me about how you manage to wrap up the books? I'm always so hopeless with paper and string.'

Florence always used paper bags, and never remembered to have seen Kattie in the shop at all, but she agreed to accompany them back to Hardborough. Kattie kept picking little bits of plants and asking her deferentially what they were. Florence had to tell her that she wasn't sure of any of them, except thyme and plantains, until the flowers began to show, and that wouldn't be for a couple of months.

One day, when the top class of the Primary School were having their free activity, which in cold weather largely meant sitting at their desks and amiably exchanging whatever dirty words they had learned lately, a stranger appeared at the door.

'You needn't rise from your seats, children. I'm the Inspector.'

'No, you're not,' said the head boy.

Mrs Traill, who had been checking the attendance register, came back to the classroom. 'I don't think I know you,' she said.

'Mrs Traill? My name is Sheppard. Perhaps you'd care to glance at my certificate of appointment from the Education Authority, which entitles me, under the Shops Act of 1950, to enter any school in which I have reasonable cause to believe that children employed in any capacity in a shop are at present being educated.'

'Employed!' cried Mrs Traill. 'I daresay they'd like to be employed, but outside of family business and newspaper rounds, I'd like you to tell me what there is for them. You might like to try again at potato-lifting time. I don't remember your ever coming here before, by the way.'

'Due to staff shortages, our visits have not been as regular as we should like.'

'Who suggested that you should come here this time?' the headmistress asked. Receiving no answer, she added. 'There's only Christine Gipping who works regularly after school.'

'At what address?'

'The Old House Bookshop. Stand up, Christine.'

The Inspector checked his notebook. 'As I expect you're aware, I have the right to examine this girl as I think fit in respect to matters under the Shops Act.'

A storm of whistling broke out from the class.

'I've brought a lady colleague with me' said the Inspector grimly. 'She's just outside, checking the car's properly locked.'

'There won't be criminal interference, then,' the head boy said placidly.

Christine was unperturbed. She followed the female inspector, who hurried in, with explanatory gestures, from the yard, into the small room behind the piano where the dinner money was counted.

To: Mrs Florence Green, The Old House Bookshop

The Education Authority's Inspectors have examined Christine Gipping and have required her to sign a declaration of truth of the matters respecting which she was examined. Although there is no suggestion of irregularity in her school attendance, it appears that consequent to the arrival of a best-selling book she worked more than 44 hours in your establishment during one week of her holidays. Furthermore her health safety and welfare are at risk in your premises which are haunted in an objectionable manner. I

96

quote from a deposition by Christine Gipping to the effect that 'the rapper doesn't come on so loud now, but we can't get rid of him altogether'. I am advised that under the provisions of the Act the supernatural would be classed with bacon-slicers and other machinery through which young persons must not be exposed to the risk of injury.

From: Mrs Florence Green

The Shop Acts which you quote only apply to young persons between the ages of fourteen and sixteen. Christine Gipping is just eleven, or what would she be doing in the Primary?

To: Mrs Florence Gipping, The Old House Bookshop

If Christine Gipping is, as you say, 11 years of age she is not permitted by law to serve in any retail business except a stall or moveable structure consisting of a board supported by trestles which is dismantled at the end of the day.

From: Mrs Florence Green

There is no room on the pavement of Hardborough High Street for boards supported by trestles to be dismantled at the end of the day. Christine, like a large proportion of the Primary School population of Suffolk, is, as you very well know, 'helping out'. She will be taking her 11+ in July and I expect her to proceed to Flintmarket Grammar School, when she will have no time for odd jobs after school.

No more was heard from the Authority's inspectors, and this complaint, wherever it had originated, died away like the earlier ones into silence. A brief note of congratulation came round from Mr Brundish. How could he have heard about it? He recalled that in his grandfather's day the Inspector had always come round the schools with a ferret in his pocket, ready to be of use in getting rid of the rats.

But the Old House Bookshop, like a patient whose crisis is over, but who cannot regain strength, showed less encouraging returns. This was to be expected in the months after Christmas. There would be more capital in hand after the warehouse was demolished and she could sell the site. Wilkins was being very slow, however. He had never been a speedy man, and of course the cold weather was against him. These old places looked as though they'd come down at a touch, but they could be stubborn. Florence was obliged to repeat this to the bank manager, who had asked her to step in for a chat, and had then asked her if she had noted how very little working capital she had at present.

'You are converting the oyster warehouse from a fixed into a current asset?'

'It isn't either at the moment,' Florence replied. 'Wilkins says the mortar's harder than the flint.'

Mr Keble observed that it was not a very favourable moment, perhaps, for selling a small building site which had always been known to be waterlogged. Florence didn't recall his having mentioned this when her loan had first been discussed.

'Rather less activity, I think, in your business at the moment? Perhaps it's just as well. At one point it seemed as though you were going to jolt us out of our old ways altogether. But all small businesses have their ups and downs. That's another thing you find easier to grasp in a position like mine, where you can take the broader view.'

Later that spring, Mrs Gamart's nephew, the member for

the Longwash Division, a brilliant, successful, and stupid young man, got his Private Bill through its first and second reading. It was an admirable bill from the point of view of his career. The provisions were acceptable to all parties – humanitarian, democratic, a contribution to the growing problem of leisure, and unlikely ever to be put into practice. Referred to as the Access to Places of Educational Value and Interest Bill, it empowered local councils to purchase compulsorily, and subject to agreed compensation, any buildings wholly or partly erected before 1549 and not used for residential purposes, provided there was no building of similar date on public show in the area. The buildings acquired were to be used for the cultural recreation of the public. Florence noticed a small paragraph about this in *The Times*, but knew that it could not affect her. Neither Hardborough nor Flintmarket councils had money for projects of any kind, and in any case, the Old House was in use for 'residential purposes' – she was still living there, although the words deflected her thoughts to the problems of upkeep. The winter had taken a large number of pegged tiles off the roof of the Old House, and a patch of damp was spreading across the bedroom ceiling, inch by inch, just as the sea was eating away the coast. There was more damp in the stock cupboard underneath the staircase. But it was the home of her books and herself, and they would remain there together.

The subject of the Bill had not been suggested to her nephew by Mrs Gamart, although she was gratified when he told her, over lunch at the House, that the idea had come to him at that party of hers last spring. As a source of energy in a place like Hardborough which needed so little, an energy, too, which was often expended in complaints, she was bound to create a widening circle of after-effects which went far beyond the original impulse. Whenever she realized this she was pleased, both for herself and for the sake of others, because she always acted in the way she felt to be right. She did not know that morality is seldom a safe guide for human conduct.

She smiled at her nephew over the lunch table, and said that she would not have the fish. 'I'm afraid living in Hardborough spoils you for fish anywhere else,' she said. 'You get it so fresh down there.' She was a very charming woman, well-preserved too, and had come up to London that day to press for some charitable scheme, nothing at all do to with the Old House Bookshop. Her nephew could not quite call to mind what it was, but he would be reminded.

9

At Hardborough Primary School the eleven-plus exam was not marked in the usual way by the headmistress herself, after the children had gone home. The papers were exchanged with Saxford Tye Primary. This gave the necessary guarantee of impartiality to the closely observant little town, or, as Mrs Traill put it, saved her from being torn to pieces after it was over. She was, perhaps, not quite so sensitive in the matter of giving out the results. The acceptances from Flintmarket Grammar School came in square white envelopes. Those from the Technical came in long buff-coloured ones. Each child in the top form, when they arrived at school that summer's morning, looked at their own desk, saw their envelopes, and knew their destiny at once. So, too, did everyone else in the class.

Hardborough children, looking back in future years over a long life, would remember nothing more painful or more decisive than the envelopes waiting on the desks. Outside it was fine weather. Yellow gorse was in flower from end to end of the common. Summer had also invaded the classroom. The pupils had been asked to bring in some Nature for the elementary biology class. There were jam-jars of white campion, dog-roses and catchfly; loose straw was scattered on the teacher's desk, and on the window-sill an eel was swimming uncomfortably in a glass tank.

It was all over in a minute. Christine was one of the last into school. She looked at her envelope and knew at once that it was what she had always expected. She had a long buff one.

Mrs Gipping called round herself to the Old House Bookshop – a concession worth noting since, with her busy day, she emerged only when she thought it strictly necessary. She had come to tell Florence that Christine would not be working for her any more, but she saw at once that Florence realized this and there was no need to deliver the message. Instead, they sat down together in the backhouse. The shop was shut, and this year's holiday-makers could be heard faintly calling from the beach.

'The old rapper doesn't seem to manifest while I'm here,' Mrs Gipping remarked. 'That knows not to waste its time, I dare say.'

'I haven't heard it so much lately,' said Florence, and then remembering the vintage marrow, she suggested they might have a drink together. 'Let's have a glass of cherry brandy, Mrs Gipping. I never do, certainly not in the afternoon, but perhaps just today.'

She took down two small glasses and the bottle, which like many liqueur bottles was of a strange shape, defiantly waisted and curved, and demanding to be kept for special occasions only.

'You got that in the church raffle, I suppose,' said Mrs Gipping. 'It's been in three years without anyone drawing the ticket. The Vicar won't know what to do without it.'

Perhaps it would bring luck. Each of the two women took a sip of the bright red, terribly sickly liquid.

'They say Prince Charles is fond of this.'

'At his age!' Then, knowing that it was her duty, as hostess, to come to the point, Florence said, 'I was very sorry to hear about Christine.'

'She's the first of ours not to get to the Grammar. It's what we call a death sentence. I've nothing against the Technical, but it just means this: what chance will she ever have of meeting and marrying a white-collar chap? She won't ever be able to look above a labouring chap or even an unemployed chap and believe me, Mrs Green, she'll be pegging out her own washing until the day she dies.'

The image of Wally flitted through Florence's tired mind. Wally had been at the Grammar this past year, and it couldn't be denied that he had been seen about lately with a new girl friend, also at the Grammar. He was teaching her to swim. 'Christine is very quick and handy,' she said, trying for a brighter view. 'And very musical,' she added, remembering the dance at the Court of King Herod. 'She's sure to make something of her life, wherever she is.'

'I don't want you to think that anything's being held against you,' said Mrs Gipping. 'That's what I principally came to say. We none of us believe that Christine would have got her eleven plus, even if she hadn't worked here after school. More than that, it may turn out to be an advantage. Experience must count. The school-leavers all say, they won't take us without experience, but how do we set about getting it? But Christine, if she needs a reference, we tell her that she's only got to come to you for it.'

'Certainly. She only has to ask.'

'She doesn't want to give up earning altogether while she's at the Technical.'

'Of course not.'

'We've been looking around a bit. We reckon she might get taken on as a Saturday girl at that new bookshop at Saxford Tye.'

Mrs Gipping spoke with a kind of placid earnestness. She finished her cherry brandy in a way that showed that she knew very well how to make a small glass last a long time.

'That's disagreeably sweet,' she said. 'Still, you can't complain if it's for the church.'

After Mrs Gipping had gone, Florence took her car out of its garage in a disused boat-shed next to the Coastguards and drove over to Saxford Tye. She parked in the main street and walked quietly about in the dusk. It was quite true. In a

103

good position, next to the smartened-up Washford Arms, there was a new bookshop.

It had not been open long, so it could not account by itself for her diminished trade. She allowed the latest Trial Balance, hovering unpleasantly on the threshold of her mind, to come in and declare itself. In those days, the separate pounds, shillings and pence allowed three separate kinds of menace from their three unyielding columns. Purchases £95 10s. 6d, (far too high), cash sales £62 10s. 11¾d, wages 12s. 6d., general expenses £2 8s. 2d., no orders, returns inward £2 17s. 6d., cash in hand £102 0s. 4d., value of stock July 31 say £600, petty cash, as usual, inexplicable. The holiday-makers had not seemed to have so much to spend this year, or perhaps not so much to spend on books. In future, if they stopped at Saxford on the way through, there might be even less.

Although she had no way of knowing this, Saxford Tye Books was not an enterprise like her own, but an investment on behalf of the simple-minded Lord Gosfield, who had sallied out from his fen-bound castle to attend Mrs Gamart's party more than a year ago. Since that time, all his acquaintances seemed to be turning their spare cottages into holiday homes, and his first slow intention (since he owned a good deal of Saxford Tye) had been to do the same thing, but then that had proved impracticable, because no one had ever yet been known to spend a holiday there. Sunk between silos and piles of root vegetables, the village was unique in that part of Suffolk in not having even a picturesque church to offer the visitor. The church had, in fact, been carelessly burnt down during the celebrations of 1925, when the Sugar Beet Subsidy Act had been passed, saving the lethargic population from extinction. But the construction of a new main road had made the Gosfield Arms, which had two good coach yards, a reasonable stopping place for motorists on the way to Hardborough or Yarmouth. The adjoining properties could be developed as shops, and Lord Gosfield seemed to remember Violet Gamart, who, mind you, was a clever woman, saying something about a bookshop. He asked his agent whether this might not be a good scheme. In collusion with this agent, who had more wits about him than his master, the brewers had made it necessary for anyone who wanted to stretch their legs, in the sense of reaching the pub's shining new lavatories, to pass the side window of the new bookshop. This displayed horse-brasses and ash-trays in the shape of sugar-beets, as well as a type of novel which Florence never intended to stock. The place was still open at half-past six. Undoubtedly it would be much livelier for Christine.

'I shall miss you, Christine, and I wanted to ask you what you'd like for a present.'

'Not one of those books. Not the kind you have.'

'Well, then, what? I'm going into Flintmarket tomorrow. What about a cardigan?'

'I'd rather have the money.' Christine was implacable. She could only find relief in causing pain. Her resentment was directed against everyone who had to do with books, and reading, and made it a condition of success to write little compositions, and to know which picture was the odd one out. She hated them all. Mrs Green, who was supposed to understand these things, and had always told her she would pass, was no better than the rest of them. She wouldn't pay them the compliment of distinguishing between them.

'Well, I hope you'll come round to the shop and see me sometimes, in the evenings.'

'I shan't have that much time.'

'The school bus gets in about five, doesn't it? I could keep a look out for you?'

'Oh, I shouldn't strain yourself. They say it's not good for you after you've turned forty.'

Perhaps it wasn't. Florence had noticed one or two eccentricities in herself lately, which might be the result of hard work, or of age, or of living alone. When the letters came, for example, she often found herself wasting time in looking at the postmarks and wondering whoever they could be from, instead of opening them in a sensible manner and finding out at once.

The letters, however, were fewer, and her whole business life might be said to be contracting. The lending library, which after all had been a steady if modest source of income, was now closed for good. This was because for the first time in its history a Public Library has been established in Hardborough. The borough had been requesting this service for very many years, and it would be difficult to say who was to be congratulated on forcing the measure through the County Council at last. The new Library was an important amenity. Fortunately, suitable premises were available. The property acquired was that of Deben's wet fish shop.

The rapper made itself heard less frequently, although once Florence found the account books, on which she spent so much time nowadays, thrown violently face downwards on to the ground. The pages were scrawled and tangled. She felt somewhat awkward in showing them to Jessie Welford's niece, who, however, told her that she was afraid other arrangements would have to be made, as she'd been given promotion at the office and wouldn't have time in the future to give a hand at the Old House. A certain coldness reflected the feeling at Rhoda's. Only just at the end, when she was making sure that she hadn't left anything behind, did she relent a little.

'Of course, my business was only to check the transactions, and I should professionally be quite wrong to offer you any other advice – '

'If it would be quite wrong, my dear, I certainly mustn't

let you do it,' said Florence, watching the assured young woman settle and pat herself into her raincoat.

'Well, then, so that seems to be all. I hope I haven't left you with any of my goods and chattels. What was it my father used to say – if you're down in the mouth think of Jonah – he came out all right.'

She was having supper next door at Rhoda's, and hurried away, leaving Florence with these images of disaster and shipwreck. Fortunately there was the spring cleaning to do, and the mailing list, which the scouts had undertaken to do for her on their hand printing-press. It would mean getting up an hour or two earlier in the mornings. She looked with shame at the rows of patiently waiting unsold books.

'You're working too hard, Florence,' Milo said.

'I try to concentrate – Put those down, they've only just come in and I haven't checked them. Surely you have to succeed, if you give everything you have.'

'I can't see why. Everyone has to give everything they have eventually. They have to die. Dying can't be called a success.'

'You're to young to bother about dying,' said Florence, feeling that this was expected of her.

'Perhaps. I believe Kattie might die, though. She wastes so much energy.'

Three times a week, Florence thought. She sighed. 'How is Kattie?' she asked.

'I don't know. As a matter of fact, Kattie has left me. She's gone to live with someone else, in Wantage. He's in Outside Broadcasting. I'm confiding in you.'

'I expect you've told everybody else in Hardborough who'll listen to you.'

'It concerns you particularly, because I shall have so much more free time. I shall be able to work here part-time as your assistant. I expect you miss that little girl.'

Florence refused to be taken aback. 'Christine learned a

great deal while she was here,' she said, 'and she had quite a nice manner with the customers.'

'Not as nice as mine,' said Milo. 'She hit Violet Gamart, didn't she? I shouldn't do that. How much can you pay me?'

'I gave Christine twelve and six a week, and I don't feel able to offer any more than that at the moment.' Surely that would get rid of Milo, although Florence was quite fond of him. If everyone was like this at the television place at Shepherd's Bush, they must find it difficult to get anything done at all. They must all be persuading each other.

'If you're interested in the work' – we used to call it 'nosey' at Müller's, she thought – 'you're welcome to come in the afternoons and try the job for a few weeks. If you don't need the twelve and sixpence you can give it to the Lifeboat or the Coastguards' box. Only please remember that I didn't ask you to come. You asked yourself.'

When Parliament reassembled, the Private Bill brought in by the member for the Longwash Division passed its third reading and went straight to the Lords. It attracted even less attention this time. Very few of the great public in whose name it was promoted read any of its amended provisions. The ancient buildings, for example, were to be subject to compulsory purchase even if they were occupied at the moment, provided they had stood vacant at any time in the past for more than five years. Mrs Gamart's nephew had had the assistance of Parliamentary draftsmen. It was impossible to say who was responsible for this detail or that.

Everybody thought it was very obliging of young Mr North to help out at the Old House, particularly when the business was not doing nearly as well as it used to. It was regrettable, perhaps, that whenever Florence had to drive over to Flint-market to see if the new orders had arrived, he immediately shut up shop and could be seen sitting in the comfortable chair, moved forward into the patch of afternoon sunlight which came through the front window. But if business was slack, how could you blame him? And he always had a book of poetry, or something of the kind, open in front of him.

As Milo never remembered on these occasions to lock the backhouse door, Christine was able to come straight in, approaching on soundless feet, wearing her new school blazer.

'Shower down thy love, O burning bright! for one
    night or the other night
Will come the Gardener in white, and gathered
    flowers are dead, Christine.'

'You watch it, Mr North,' said Christine.

'What unpleasant expressions they teach you in that new school of yours!'

Christine turned very red.

'I didn't come here to mix it with your sort,' she said.

A kind of unease had brought her back and she was disappointed not to find Florence there, partly so that she could cheer her up a little, partly so that she could show that she wouldn't take the job on again at any price. Also, she might as well show her the cardigan which she had bought with the money she had been given. It buttoned up high, not like the old-fashioned sort.

'Why don't you help Mrs Green any more?' Milo asked. 'She misses you.'

'Well, she's got you, hasn't she, Mr North? You're always in and out.'

Hesitating, not wanting to seem to ask for information, she burst out: 'They say they won't let her go on keeping this bookshop.'

'Who are "they"?'

'They want the Old House for something else they've thought of.'

'Why should you mind about that, my dear?'

'They say she can't hold on to it, do they'll have her up. That'll mean County Court. She'll have to swear to tell the whole truth and nothing but the truth.'

'We must hope that it won't come to that.'

Christine hardly felt that she had reasserted her position as yet. She minced round, dusting here and there – the duster needed a wash, as usual, she said – and looking with a stranger's recognition at her old acquaintances on the shelves.

'These don't ought to be with the Stickers,' she said, heaving up the two volumes of the *Shorter Oxford Dictionary*.

'No one has offered to buy them.'

'Still, they're not Stickers. They're a stock line.'

There was nothing much more to do. Even now, at the end of the day, there was scarcely anything that needed putting to rights.

'I don't see so much wrong with this shop, give it's terribly damp, and you can't tell when the rapper'll start up.'

'Certainly there can't be much wrong with it, or I shouldn't be here.'

'How long are you going to stay, then?'

'I don't know. I might not have the energy to stay much longer.'

'You might not have the energy to get up and go,' said Christine, watching him, with scornful fascination, where he sat. It would do him good to get a bit of garden and work it, she thought, even if it was only a couple of rows of radishes.

'I never had time to sit about when I was assistant.'

'I'm sure you didn't. You're either a child or a woman, and neither of them have any idea how to relax.'

'You watch it,' said Christine.

10

The cold weather came on early after the fine summer of 1960. By the beginning of October Raven had begun to speak pessimistically about the cattle, who were coughing piteously. In the early morning the thick white vapour came up to the level of their knees, so that their bodies seemed to float detached above the mist. Their heads, with large ears at half-mast, turned slowly in a cloud of steamy breath towards the chance comer.

The mist did not lift until nearly mid-day and closed down again by four o'clock. It was madness for Mr Brundish to go out in such conditions; and yet at Holt House, entirely by himself, he was slowly getting ready to pay a visit. By a quarter to eleven he had assumed the appearance almost of a boulevardier, with a coat collared in fur, and a grey Homburg hat, rather higher in the crown than was usual in those years. The natives of Hardborough only breathed the autumn air through woollen scarves, and Mr Brundish also wore one of these, and took a stick from the many waiting in the hall.

Because of the mist, only the hat and upper three-quarters of Mr Brundish could be seen, bending down with an occasional terrifying gasp and wheeze, as he navigated the Ropewalk, the Sheepwalk and Anson Street. It was at first thought, by those at their windows, that he was heading for the doctor's, or, still more alarming, for the church. Mr Brundish had not atended a service for some years. He was pale, and seemed afflicted. It was thought that he looked very moderate.

If not the doctor's or the church, then it could only be The Stead. Improbable or impossible as it seemed, he was toiling up the front steps, and, clear of the mist at last, stood pressing the bell.

Mrs Gamart was making a morning entry in her diary, and had written *Wednesday: wretched weather for Oct. Hydrangea petolaria quite damped off.* She heard the bell and was ready to rise, making light of the interruption, when she realized who the visitor really was. Then she felt the same disbelief as the rest of Hardborough, who had watched the progress from Holt House. The young local girl who helped with the washing up and had answered the front door, looked half-stunned, as though she had witnessed trees walking.

To be accepted by this tiresome old man would be an entry into a new dimension of time and space – the past centuries of inhabited Suffolk, and its present silent and watchful existence. From the very first months of her arrival her invitations had been refused, on the steady excuse of ill-health. Yet, beyond question, there were little gatherings at Holt House, distinguished by visitors who stayed the night, as well as ancient cronies drawn from the deepest recesses of East Anglia. Men only perhaps, although it was said – but Mrs Gamart didn't believe it – that Mrs Green had been to tea, and her own husband had certainly never been included. The General, however, with the transparent complicity of the male sex, insisted that old Mr Brundish was a decent fellow. The inadequacy of this remark vexed Mrs Gamart into silence.

And now Mr Brundish had come. He made no apologies as he was shown in, for in his day none had been thought necessary for an eleven o'clock call. Without attempting to disguise his weakness, without pretending to stop for a few minutes to admire the proportions of the hall, he clung to the banisters, struggling for breath. His stick fell with a clatter to the shining floor.

'I shall recover my stick later. Fortunately I have retained all my faculties.'

Mrs Gamart, who had come out to meet him, thought it best to lead the way into the drawing-room. The sweeping French windows overlooked the sea, as misty as the land. They both sat down. Without any further reference to his health, Brundish went on:

'I have come to ask you something. That is not very good manners, but I do not know that I can put it any better. If you mind being asked, you must say so at once. I could speak to your husband, of course.'

From long habit, Mrs Gamart rejected the idea that her husband might be necessary for anything. The concentration of her visitor appeared to waver and cease. For what seemed a considerable time he sat with his eyes closed, while his face took on a curious slatey pallor, as though he had been bleached by the sea. Then he resumed:

'A curious experience, fainting. One can't tell if one is doing it properly. There is nothing to go on. One can't remember the last time. You had better offer me something,' he added loudly, and then, in precisely the same tone: 'The bitch cannot deny me a glass of brandy.'

Mrs Gamart looked doubtfully at the stricken man. If he was having some kind of attack, all that was necessary was to ring the doctor's. Then he would be taken away. He would be under an obligation, of course, as anyone must be who is taken ill in someone else's house, although Mr Brundish, she realized, might not recognize obligations. But he couldn't have made the painful transit from Holt House, on a day like this, simply to tell her that he wasn't well, unless he suddenly wanted to make amends for the short-sightedness of fifteen years. It would be better not to offer him stimulants, she thought.

'Shall I see about some coffee?' she asked.

'The woman is trying to poison me. The moment will

pass.' Mr Brundish opened and closed his hands, as though to grasp the air, yet even in that movement there was nobility. 'I want you to leave Florence Green alone,' he brought out.

Mrs Gamart was utterly taken aback. 'Did she ask you to come here?'

'Not at all. She is simply a woman, no longer young, who wants to keep a bookshop.'

'If Mrs Green has any cause to complain,' said Mrs Gamart, 'I suppose she could employ a solicitor. I believe that she is rather given to changing her legal advisers.'

'Why do you want her out of that house? I live in an oldish house myself, and I know how inconvenient they are. The bookshop is draughty, ineligible for a second mortgage, and, of course, haunted.'

Tact and good training had by this time come to Mrs Gamart's assistance.

'Hasn't it occurred to you, as someone who must care so much for the welfare and the heritage of this place, that a building of such historical interest could be put to a better use?'

This was a false move. Mr Brundish didn't care at all about the welfare or the heritage of Hardborough. He *was*, in a sense, Hardborough; it never occurred to him whether he cared or not.

'Old age is not the same thing as historical interest,' he said. 'Otherwise we should both of us be more interesting than we are.'

Mrs Gamart had realized by now that though her visitor might be conducting the conversation according to some kind of rules, they were not the ones she knew. Some different kind of defence would accordingly be needed.

'I say again, I want you to leave my friend Florence Green alone,' shouted Mr Brundish. 'Alone!'

'Your friend, you know, seems to have fallen foul of the

law, I rather think more than once. If that is the case, I, of course, can have nothing to say. If she goes on as she has begun, the law will have to take its course.'

'I don't know whether you are referring to a law that wasn't in existence a year ago, and crawled through Parliament while our backs were turned? I'm talking about an order for compulsory purchase. You may call it an eviction. That is a fairer term. Did you put your precious nephew up to that Private Bill of his?'

She would not lower herself so far as to pretend not to understand. 'It's true that my nephew's Bill may affect the bookshop, as there's a provision that the premises must have stood empty for five years. That would certainly apply to the Old House.' How had he come by this information? It seemed as though he had drawn it in through unseen roots, without moving from Holt House, without seeing or listening. 'There are so many authorities to consider, you know, Mr Brundish. Ordinary mortals like myself – ' she hesitated – 'and you, would scarcely know where to begin. I'm on the bench, and fairly well used to public service, but I should be quite out of my depth. We shouldn't even be able to find the right person to write to.'

'I know perfectly well, madam, who to write to. Over the past years, if I hadn't made it my business to know, I should have lost several hundred acres of my marshes, some farming land, and two pumping mills. Let me inform you that the purchaser of the Old House will have to be the Flintmarket Borough Council, and that they will proceed under the Acquisition of Land Authorisation Procedure Act of 1946, the Housing Act of 1957, and this grotesque effort of your nephew's. If nothing has been done so far, we can make common front against them. If notice has been served that they are willing to treat, we must call for a private hearing in front of a government inspector.'

The significance and weight of that 'we' could not be

115

mistaken. Violet Gamart perfectly understood the bargain that was being offered. An alliance was proposed, a working alliance at any rate, between Holt House and The Stead, and in return something was demanded which in fact she had no power to bring about. But did that matter? She would temporize. Mr Brundish would have to call again to undertake further persuasion, she must call on him to discuss details. His mind was not under complete control, he would forget what had been said last time, he would become a regular visitor. She would have yielded nothing and gained considerably. Meanwhile it would be wiser not to promise too much.

'We could certainly think of ways of making the move easier, if it has to come. There are still plenty of other shops to let, you know, in larger towns than Hardborough.'

'That's not what I am talking about! You must talk about what I am talking about! It was difficult for me to get here in this weather! – Either this woman is stupid, or else she is malevolent.'

'I wish I could do more.'

'I am to understand, then, that you will do nothing.'

This was exactly what she had meant, and what she intended. She had to restore the situation, and neither evasion nor frankness would answer; he saw through both of them. That frightful old men have hearts ready to be touched was, however, something that she had never questioned. She turned on him a delightful smile, which warmed her dark bright eyes and had moved many more important people than him.

'But you mustn't speak to me like that, Mr Brundish. You can't realize what you are saying. You must think me outrageous. Is that it?'

Mr Brundish gave the impression of carefully turning the words over in his mind, as though they were pebbles of which he must ascertain the value.

'I find that I cannot answer either "yes" or "no". By "outrageous" I take it that you mean "unexpectedly offensive". Certainly you have been offensive, Mrs Gamart, but you have been exactly as I expected.'

With some difficulty he rose, and propping himself on the various bits of furniture, not all of them adapted to bear his weight, he regained his hat and left The Stead. But half-way across the street – the mist having cleared by this time, so that he could be clearly seen by the inhabitants of Hardborough – Mr Brundish fell over and died.

The local tradespeople, in consultation with the Flintmarket Chamber of Commerce, decided not to close on the day of old Mr Brundish's funeral. It was market day, and there would be a fair chance of extra sales.

'I'm not going to close either,' Florence told Raven, who on occasion acted as sexton. Raven was surprised, because in his view she had a right to go to the ceremony, being able to claim better acquaintance with the deceased than many who'd be there. This was true, but she could not explain to him how much she wanted to be by herself, to think about her strange correspondent and champion. On what uncanny errand had he crossed the square, with his hat and stick, that day?

He was buried in the flinty soil of the churchyard among the Suffolk sea dead, midshipmen drowned at eleven years old, fishermen lost with all hands. The northeast corner of the acre was the family plot of the earth-loving Brundishes. Hardborough, huddled below the level of its marshes, was for one day at least a centre of interest. Who would have thought that old Mr Brundish would have known so many people, and that so many relatives would have turned up, and such a lot from London? He was a Fellow of the Royal Society, it seemed; how had that come about? The public houses had all applied for an extension, and there was a large cold lunch at The Stead, where the guests talked and laughed, and then subdued their laughs, and scarcely knew where to put them. It was known that the old man had died intestate, and Mr Drury had set out on the prolonged research which would dispose of Holt House and the marshes and pumping mills and the £2,705 13s. 7d. remaining in the current account.

While the church ceremony was still in progress, and Florence, without any expectation of customers, was slowly winding down the cash register, General Gamart came into the shop. He stood for a moment blocking the light. Then, evidently giving himself a command, he took three paces forward. At first, that seemed to exhaust the whole enterprise. He was speechless, and fidgeted with a pile of Noddy annuals. Florence Green did not much feel like helping him. He had not been in the shop for some months, and she presumed that he had been acting under orders. Then she relented, knowing that he had come on a kind impulse. In the end, she valued kindness above everything.

'You don't want a book, do you?'

'Not exactly. I just came in to say "A good man gone".'

The General cleared his throat. It was the best he could do. 'I believe you knew Edmund Brundish quite well,' he added hoarsely.

'I feel as though I did, but when I come to think of it, I've only spoken to him during one afternoon in my whole life.'

'Well, I've never spoken to the fellow at all. He was in the first show, of course, but not in the Suffolks, he was in the RFC, I believe – he wanted to fly. Odd, that.'

The General talked much more freely now that the sticky part, the condolences, were over.

'Another odd thing, he was calling on us that very morning.'

'He wanted to speak to your wife, I suppose.'

'Yes, you're quite right. Violet told me all about it. He

118

made a great effort to call on her, it seems, to congratulate her on her idea – her idea, I mean, about this Arts Centre. I'm sorry I didn't manage to get a word with him myself. I must say I shouldn't have thought Art was quite his line of country, but, well, a good man gone. Twelve years older than I am. I suppose any of us could collapse like that, when you come to think of it.'

There was nothing to stop him going on like this indefinitely. 'You mustn't be late for lunch, General Gamart.' She knew about the preparations at The Stead. He would be needed to open the wine.

Conscious of some want of tact, half relieved and half dissatisfied, he dismissed himself and withdrew.

A month or so later, the Old House was requisitioned under the new Act of Parliament. Since one of the provisions was that there should be no other uninhabited buildings of the same date in the area, the oyster warehouse could have been offered in its place, so it was unfortunate that Florence had given orders to have it pulled down. Wilkins had taken nearly a year over the demolition, but he was going ahead quite fast now.

Large numbers of pieces of paper were put through the brass letter-box of the bookshop. The postman apologized for bringing so many. On one of them the City of Flintmarket notified Florence Mary Green that they required to purchase and take under the provisions of the Act of 1959 or Acts or parts of Acts incorporated in the above Acts the lands or hereditaments mentioned and described in the schedule as delineated in the plan attached hereto (but they had forgotten to attach it) and thereon coloured pink, together with all mines and minerals in and under the said lands, other than coal, and that they were willing to treat with you and each and every of you for the purchase of the said lands and as to the compensation to be made to you and each and every of

119

you by reason of the taking of the said lands authorized as aforesaid. Florence felt, as she read this, that it was the moment for the rapper to manifest itself, and when it did not, she almost missed it.

The notice also appeared in the *Flintmarket, Kingsgrave, and Hardborough Times*, making poor Florence feel like a wanted criminal. It was certainly not her imagination that old acquaintances avoided her in the street, and customers wore a surprised expression, saying, Oh, I thought I saw somewhere that you had closed down. Mr Thornton, Mr Drury and Mr Keble and their wives no longer came to the shop at all, for it was tainted.

She didn't mind so much as she had expected. It was defeat, but defeat is less unwelcome when you are tired. The compensation would be enough to pay off the bank loan and to put down a deposit on a rented property, perhaps somewhere quite else. Change should be welcome. And after all, as she now realized, Mr Brundish himself had come round to the idea of the new Centre. For some reason, this idea gave her more pain than the notice of Willingness to Treat.

Raven, in the bar of the Anchor, wanted to know how that lot at Flintmarket Town hall, who according to themselves never had a penny to spare, and couldn't even afford to drain their own marshes, had managed to raise the money to buy out Mrs Green at the Old House. But Flintmarket Urban District Council were no more ready to discuss their finances than any other public body. The Recreation Committee said in their report how heartening it was, that if anything was truly wanted and needed, a benefactor could always be found to step forward and make it possible.

Florence's solicitors in Flintmarket were at first greatly excited at the idea of handling, as they called it, one of the first cases under a new Act. They spoke of bringing an action for declaration, or applying for an order of *certiorari*.

'Would that do any good?'

'Well, there can't really be any legal grounds for challenging an administrative decision, but it's been held that in fact the public can do so, on the grounds of natural justice.'

'What is natural justice?' asked Florence.

After the solicitors found that their client had very little money, they gave up the order of *certiorari* and discussed the matter of compensation. Like all her other advisers, they took a gloomy and hostile view. There would be no claim for depreciation, as books were legally counted as ironmongery, as not losing value by being moved about. Nothing could be claimed for services, as it was a one-man business. Mr Thornton would have made a joke about its being a 'one-woman' business, but the Flintmarket solicitors did not do so. There remained the issue of compensation for the Old House itself.

When, after a few more weeks, she rang them up, they spoke of snags and delays. By this they meant, although they did not admit it for some time, that she was unlikely to get anything at all. Various Town and Country Planning Acts provided that if a house was so damp that it was unfit for human habitation and subsidence was threatened, no claim for compensation could be made.

'But the Old House has been there for centuries without subsiding. I'm inhabiting it, and I'm still human, and it's not as damp as all that – it dries out in the summer, and in midwinter. And anyway, what about the land?'

The solicitor referred to the land as 'the cleared site value', as though the Old House had already ceased to exist.

'That can only be estimated if it is in fact land, but an inspection of the cellars has established that the property is standing in half an inch of water.'

'What inspection? I wasn't notified about it.'

'Apparently on various dates when you were absent from the business, an experienced builder and plasterer, Mr John

121

Gipping, was sent in by the council to make an estimate of the condition of the walls and cellar.'

'John Gipping!'

'Of course, we assume that he made a peaceable entry.'

'I'm sure he did. He's not at all a violent man. What I should like to know is, who let him in?'

'Oh, your assistant, Mr Milo North. It will be assumed that he acted as your servant, and following your instructions. Have you any comments?'

'Only that I'm glad they gave the job to Gipping. He hasn't found it easy to get work lately.'

'What makes it very awkward for us is that Mr North has also signed a deposition to the effect that the damp state of the property has affected his health, and made him unfit for ordinary employment.'

'Why did you do it?' she asked Milo. 'Did somebody ask you to?'

'They did ask me rather often, and it seemed the easiest thing to do.'

Milo no longer came round to help in the bookshop; she happened to meet him crossing the common. He made no attempt to avoid her on this occasion. Indeed, he tried to make himself useful by suggesting that if she still wanted an assistant, Christine might well be free again, since, after only half a term at the Technical, she had been suspended by the headmaster. Milo said that he did not know the details, and Florence did not press for them.

There was not very much more that she could do. The bank manager, with some embarrassment, asked her if it would be convenient for her to make an appointment to see him as soon as possible. He wanted to know whether what he had heard was correct, that she had no legal right to compensation, and, in that case, what she intended to do about repayment of the loan.

'I was hoping to start again,' said Florence. 'I thought I could.'

'I should not advise you to try another small business. It's curious how many people look upon the bank as no more than a charitable institution. There comes a time when each of us must be content to call it a day. There is, of course, always the stock. If that could be liquidated, we should be well on the way out of our difficulty.'

'You mean that you want me to sell the books?'

'To clear off the loan, yes – the books and your car. I fear that will be absolutely necessary.'

Florence was left, therefore, without a shop and without books. She had kept, it is true, two of the Everymans, which had never been very good sellers. One was Ruskin's *Unto this Last*, the other was Bunyan's *Grace Abounding*. Each had its old bookmarker in it, *Everyman I will be thy guide, in thy most need to go by thy side*, and the Ruskin also had a pressed gentian, quite colourless. The book must have gone, perhaps fifty years before, to Switzerland in springtime.

In the winter of 1960, therefore, having sent her heavy luggage on ahead, Florence Green took the bus into Flintmarket via Saxford Tye and Kingsgrave. Wally carried her suitcases to the bus stop. Once again the floods were out, and the fields stood all the way, on both sides of the road, under shining water. At Flintmarket she took the 10.46 to Liverpool Street. As the train drew out of the station she sat with her head bowed in shame, because the town in which she had lived for nearly ten years had not wanted a bookshop.

123

PENELOPE FITZGERALD

Offshore

Winner of the Booker Prize

'This is an astonishing book. Hardly more than 50,000 words, it is written with a manic economy that makes it seem even shorter, and with a tamped-down force that continually explodes in a series of exactly controlled detonations. It is funny, its humour far more robust than it at first appears, but it has in addition a sense of battles lost, of happiness at any rate brushed by the fingers as it passes by, of understanding gained at the last second. *Offshore* is a marvellous achievement: strong, supple, humane, ripe, generous and graceful.' Bernard Levin *Sunday Times*

Human Voices

'One of the pleasures of reading Penelope Fitzgerald is the unpredictability of her intelligence, which never loses its quality, but springs constant surprises, and if you make the mistake of reading her fast because she is so readable, you will miss some of the best jokes. I wish it were longer . . . for it is certainly a very funny novel about the BBC, and that in itself is an occasion for joy.' Michael Ratcliffe *The Times*

Flamingo

Penelope Fitzgerald

The Beginning of Spring

Frank Reid is an Englishman living in Moscow earning his living as the owner of a small print works. As the novel opens his wife, Nellie, leaves him without explanation and travels back to London. From that moment until her very last sentence, the author draws a majestic emotional arc; and under it, the life of the Reid household, the expatriate community, Frank's colleagues, friends and children, the Russians with whom he comes into contact – all the mesmerising multiplicity of life which Penelope Fitzgerald can so peerlessly depict over such a short space. The life of the city itself, swirling around them all, hardly aware of the upheaval that is about to break upon it, is as authentic a transportation as any in contemporary fiction.

'Scrupulously well written, subtle in is effects, and feels completely authentic. *The Beginning of Spring* opens out into something more than you might expect.'

Hermione Lee, *The Observer*

Flamingo

Penelope Fitzgerald

Innocence

'I know of no one who expresses so deftly and entertainingly the way in which life seldom turns out as expected. A wonderful book.'   John Jolliffe, *Spectator Books of the Year*

'This is by far the fullest and richest of Penelope Fitzgerald's novels, and also the most ambitious. Her writing, as ever, has a natural authority, is very funny, warm and gently ironic, and full of tenderness towards human beings and their bravery in living.'
Anne Duchene, *Times Literary Supplement*

'*Innocence* wields a curious fascination, replete with the sense of sleepy, slightly anxious fatalism that pervades much of the Italian cinema of the period. Its magic, and its message, are as oblique and inconclusive as the lives of its characters, but both have a lingering power, refreshingly fictive, deliciously un-English.'   Jan Dalley, *Literary Review*

Flamingo

J. G. Farrell

Troubles

J. G. Farrell's brilliant evocation of Ireland in turmoil and the British Empire in decline.

'Subtly modulated, richly textured, sad, funny and altogether memorable.' *The Times Literary Supplement*

'A tour de force . . . sad, tragic, also very funny.' *Guardian*

The Singapore Grip

'A brilliantly idiosyncratic and funny novel . . . Farrell's imagination is remarkable for its depth and intensity . . . his relaxed prose is both ironic and warm . . . Farrell's characters are as unique as the densely imagined worlds in which they move.' *New Statesman*

The Siege of Krishnapur

Winner of the Booker Prize.

'A novel of quite outstanding quality.' *The Times*

Flamingo